THE TORTURED
SECUTOR

First Edition

Published by The Nazca Plains Corporation
Las Vegas, Nevada
2007

ISBN: 978-1-934625-33-0

Published by

The Nazca Plains Corporation ®
4640 Paradise Rd, Suite 141
Las Vegas NV 89109-8000

PUBLISHER'S NOTE

The Tortured Secutor is a work of fiction created wholly by *Jardonn
Smith's* imagination. All characters are fictional and any resemblance to
any persons living or deceased is purely by accident. No portion of this
book reflects any real person or events.

Cover, Vova Pomortzeff
Art Director, Blake Stephens

DEDICATION

To rulers who inspire their citizens, rather than abusing them.

THE TORTURED SECUTOR

First Edition

Jardonn Smith

CONTENTS

AUTHOR'S NOTE

For ease of memory, I've abandoned the standard Roman formalities of three, sometimes four names to reference one person. Other than Emperors and Generals mentioned who are real, these fictional characters are given first and last names only.

A Boner Book

THE TORTURED SECUTOR
Greetings from the Elysian Fields

Persephone enjoys our tale, so on occasion she summons us to regurgitate the waters of the River Lethe, the river of forgetfulness, and then we remember. We talk while she listens.

So here we are, together again. Good to see you, Artimos.

And you, Philo. Shall we begin at our beginning?

Of course.

Will you speak or should I?

You are the master of details, Artimos. You speak. And try not to layer it with mush.

Too emotional, am I?

At times.

Only when speaking of you. Surely you can forgive me that.

All is forgiven. Always.

Persephone fidgets. You be still. I'll begin.

A Boner Book

Ludus Magnus

I am a freeborn man, but my blood is tainted with Greek. I only mention this because some Roman patricians insist we keep records of such things. From Athens came my great-grandfather to serve as one personal physician to Emperor Trajan. My great-grandfather married Roman, as did his son and his son, which leaves me with one-eighth of Greek still flowing in my veins. Artimos is Greek, given to me with purpose, for a Greek name lends an air of credence to the profession of physician. After all, most of what we know and still use originated there. My great-grandfather's freedom came upon Trajan's death, for in the Emperor's testament coins were bestowed to him and it was decreed that he be released from servitude. As so often happens and is the right of a freedman, he took the family name of Trajan, Traius, as his own to honor the master who freed him, and so upon the city rolls of Roman citizens I am officially known as Artimos Traius.

As for the man who criticizes my speech, he knows both sides of it -- the life of a freedman and the life of a slave. His name is Philokrates. He came to Rome from Macedonia. He is called Philo.

His adulthood story of bad luck turned to good luck, with varying degrees of luck along the way officially began in A.D. 262. From the village of Veneton did he become prisoner at age 13 for stealing bread because he was hungry. Sentenced to ten years of construction labor in the building of bridges and aqueducts, he'd served eight of those ten years when his refusal to accept the advances of an enamored Roman crew leader brought a fabricated story of his attempted escape. For this he was sold at auction into slavery, and because of his finely sculptured physique built from hard labor, Philo was deemed to be of potential value as entertainment. He was put aboard ship for transport to Rome. From the barge docks on the Tiber River was he delivered in chains by horsecart at sundown to the Ludus Magnus complex in Rome, imperial gladiatorial training ground adjacent to and connected by underground tunnel with the Amphitheatrum Flavium, or if you wish, the Colosseum.

He arrived with six others. All six were in leg irons, wrist locks and neck braces connected by single chain to six necks. He arrived in filthy fabric loin cloth. He also was filthy, short-tempered and exhausted from five days kept in the heated belly of a wooden ship. He was one of three of the six who physically displayed resistance upon entry to the processing area of prison cells, and for his defiance Philo was humbled along with the other two after all men were released from their neck connector chain.

The short chains between their wrist locks were draped over spikes extending from horizontal wooden beams that supported the ceiling. Their leg-ironed bare feet dangled inches from the floor, their arms stretched overhead and close together, their bodies hung suspended in open air near the center of the room, and they were whipped -- not in a manner to cut their slave skin and lessen their property value, but merely in a manner to create pain until they stopped resisting. They were stripped naked. Their beatings came from leather straps three inches wide and three feet long, and blows were struck simultaneously from the front of them and from their backsides. Genitals were spared. Faces were spared. All else was fair game.

With gladiators watching from their cells, three new recruits were painted red with welts -- welts that would disappear in one or two days. Philo was too weary to apply logic, too overwhelmed with anger and hopelessness to consider that by grasping hold of the spike with one hand he could easily raise his wrists above the spike to release himself from suspension. Anyway, what would be the use? How far could he go with leg irons shuffling his steps? His pain was brutal, and quickly he learned that arching his spine to lessen impact from behind only further exposed his chest and belly to blows from the front, and so he hung there silently taking his punishment. He refused to cry out. Suppressing his voicebox was the only form of defiance he had to give them, and once his chin fell onto his chest and he became motionless with eyes closed, his punishment ended. The other two had long since been taken down, brought to me for examination, and then locked into the cells that would be their homes for the rest of their lives. Philo outlasted them by a good 20 minutes, and as he too was brought down from his suspended torture one of our guards said, "He's more beast than man. Give him to the physician."

That would be me. Finished with checking in three obedient and two stubborn slaves, idly had I stood throughout the remainder of Philo's beating. Thought nothing of it. Had seen it many times before, but I will confess that this particular man did attract my eye more than the others. Even though I'd already worked my day shift and stayed extra hours to handle these newcomers, even though I was agitated, weary and wanted to go home, I could not help but admire this man for his stamina and resolve. He made me wait, and he did so for a longer time than had any man before him. Most impressive, I thought.

Philo was laid upon a long table still bound in leg irons and wrist restraints. The guards put him on his back, his hands covering his naked genitals, and I instructed that he was to be washed. Philo did not resist the servants performing this task. He slept. He snored, comforts of warm water, soap and ocean sponges quickly easing the sting of leather. They left him with skin patted dry for my examination in the manner they knew I wanted him: with his arms out of my way beyond his head, shoulders to elbows on the table, forearms and hands dangling off its edge.

So deep was his slumber that he barely reacted to the touch of my manipulating fingers upon him, as I inspected his genitals, as I opened his jaw for a look at his teeth and tongue. The exploration of swab stick into his nostrils for mucus samples and ears for wax did not stir him, nor did the tapping of my reflex-testing fingers onto his chest, elbow joints, knee joints and soles of his feet. When I had him turned over for cleansing to his back side, Philo continued his dreams, perhaps thoughts of his harem of females, their delicate fingers massaging with soap his tortured muscles before drying him with soft linens. What did stir him was my attempted inspection of his rectum. When my fingers spread his butt cheeks and metal made contact with his anus, Philo bolted. He rolled from the table and tried to run, not remembering that his ankles could not run, and he fell forward, breaking his fall with bound hands.

Once again our Roman guards, a new pair coming on duty for the evening shift, seized Philo and hung him by his wrists onto the overhead spike. One stood behind Philo, clamping his hands onto Philo's thighs; the other stood in front, pounding him with fists. "No bone," said the one from behind, and the punches were concentrated on his belly. Philo's hard and stretched muscle was pounded with meaty fists from below his sternum to above his pelvis, and with no way to draw up his legs or move forward, back or side to side, Philo took these punches with nothing but muscle for defense.

He wanted to puke, but there was nothing inside his belly to puke. All he could do was tighten himself, groan upon impact, grunt upon impact, and stare past the Roman guard throwing punches into him. Guard's name? Drusus Macarius, and if ever a man could have lived his previous life as a bull and bring with him in this life these same physical traits as a human, that would be Drusus. With broad and compact chest, bulging and rounded shoulders supporting massive arms carved from central limbs of a mighty oak tree, Drusus's thick-skinned, bony-knuckled fists penetrated like a battering ram.

The method and intent of Drusus and his assistant was not one of beating the man, questioning him, and then beating him some more until he answered correctly. No, initiation to the Ludus Magnus for an obstinate slave simply involved a continuous beating until either he voluntarily begged for an end to it with promises of good behavior, or until he passed out. As Philo took a barrage of punishing blows from left and right, he gave no indication he was anywhere near the point of surrender. It was as though he intended to die before giving in. Drusus threw his arsenal of straight punches, hooks and uppercuts with precise accuracy to the left of Philo's navel, to the right, below it and above, but Philo showed no signs of weakening. With every muscle tensed from his forearms to the calves of his legs, his fists clenched and toes curled, Philo stared blankly, glassy-eyed, his mind seemingly elsewhere.

In fact, Philo's eyes, when opened and not clenched shut from pain, fixated upon me. He gazed past Drusus and concentrated on me.

Perhaps this was because I dressed differently than Drusus -- he covered with leather around his waist, sandals on his feet and nothing else; I covered in tunic of brown wool from shoulder to knee, a corded fabric belt around my waist -- but I believe that Philo more than likely saw in me a reason for hope. My expression could not lie. It saddened me that he suffered. It was my fault that he suffered, my decision to let him sleep rather than warning him of where I would touch him that brought about his second round of punishment, and I am certain Philo used my frown and the slow turn of my head left to right as his strength. I am also certain my image was the first sign of compassion shown him in many a day, and although I was mostly powerless to help him, I did have one option to use after giving Drusus and his partner a few minutes to make their point.

"Drusus, that should do for now," I interrupted while stepping towards them. "I cannot save ruptured innards. Take him to his cell. I will finish his inspection tomorrow."

Not much was left of Philo. With two guards stepping away to catch their breaths, Philo's body hung limp, head fallen back between stretched arms. He gasped for air, each exhale clearly defining the muscles of his abdomen, beaten but not broken. A sight to behold! And as a new layer of sweat brightened him with a glistening sheen, that summed up the whole of this man. He remained a man, tragic, yet majestic. Not one word had he uttered to any of us since his arrival. Not once had he begged us to stop. He had fought us with the only weapons available to him: his muscle, his strength of will, his defiance, and in that contest Philo emerged the victor.

As he was released from his suspension and carried to his cell, Philo surely heard Drusus speak to me of him, the last words remembered before he stumbled to unconsciousness laying upon stone floor, "Strong man this one is, Artimos. Nearly broke my hands."

Philo did not remain on the floor. I did not go home as I should have, but instead coaxed Drusus to help me lift Philo onto his cot, nothing more than a wood frame with hard mattress on top, mattress compacted of straw. We connected the chain between his leg irons with chain threaded through a metal ring that was bolted to foot of his cot frame.

"Thank you Drusus. Check on him every half hour. I am going home for a few hours of sleep. Then I will finish processing him. I'm finished with the other five."

I returned before sunrise, before Philo had awakened, before any of them had awakened.

"Drusus, are your fists still sore?"

"A little stiff. Do you have a salve that will help?"

"Of course. Come with me."

I admired Drusus Macarius. As a prime example of brute strength meshing with masculine beauty, no man was finer. His square head and square jaw gave him the appearance of statue carved from stone, and if ever I felt threatened by any of the slaves within this complex, Drusus was the man to call. It should also be known that he had been my chosen companion for nights of drinking and debauchery back in the times he worked day shift with me, for there was no place in the city where I could be challenged or intimidated, not as long as Drusus was by my side. And when we collapsed onto my bed in my house four blocks from our place of employment, I made certain Drusus received his reward for my protection. After all, I do have skills other than those of a physician.

"So, Drusus, how is that rock-solid, knuckle-breaking slave of ours?"

"Hasn't moved, except when I woke him up to give him a drink of water. Didn't know if you'd ever gotten around to it."

"No, I hadn't. Was he docile?"

"Never woke up, really."

"Well, stand by close. I'm going to see if his brain has any logical thought."

With Drusus outside the cell door, I stood inside beyond Philo's head where he could not see me. Still naked, laying on his back with leg irons and wrist restraints attached, the slumbering Philo captured my fascination. His well-engineered musculature was sturdy and precise. Other than the clearly visible lines where leather had struck him, everything about him was perfect. I admired this new slave not only from the perspective of a physician, but also as a man who appreciates beauty of the masculine form -- the male image as art, as dominating power, and as an object deserving of worship. Perhaps foolishly, I removed the chain securing him to bed frame, and although the clanking caused him to stir, his eyes remained closed and he settled in to continue his sleep.

"It's all right, Drusus." I moved towards the door to exit the cell. "His trainer won't be in for another hour, so I'll just let him..."

"I think we have action," Drusus interrupted while pointing to the cot. Turning quickly revealed that not only had Philo awakened but was sitting on his cot with feet on the floor as though ready to launch himself towards the door, which would also be towards me.

I spoke quickly and professionally and in Greek, attempting to avoid another of his outbursts.

"Good morning, Philokrates of Veneton." He abruptly stood with thoughts of violence against me, but then he remembered. I was the compassionate one, the one who'd ordered his torture to end, and now here I was making myself vulnerable to his attack. Of course, he did not see Drusus waiting outside the open door to protect me as always, but still Philo did not attack me. Philo sat on his mattress with feet again on the floor, now ready to listen.

"It is time for you to accept what you are and where you are. I know you are not a foolish man. Tell me I am correct in this."

"I should not be here." His first words were spoken in Greek -- his first words since arriving to the Ludus Magnus.

"But you are here. I know your history. Nothing can change that."

"Something must."

"What must change is you, Philokrates. Your anger is good, but it will not help you unless used properly. Here, you will learn to do just that. We are trained to show you how. What say you?"

Philo threw up his feet to lay on the mattress, covering his eyes with the backs of his hands. For the doctor he would suppress his anger. For me, for now, Philo would obey. "I am not a foolish man."

"Good. Now, we start anew. My name is Artimos Traius."

"You're Greek?"

"Little. My great grandfather was brought here from Athens. He was physician to Emperor Trajan. He was given his freedom upon Trajan's death, but Emperor Hadrian suggested he come here to work for salary tending to gladiators. It is unwise to defy the wishes of Emperors, and so here we have been ever since. That Greek married Roman, as did his son and my father."

"And you?"

"I have made no such commitments." A horrific rumble echoed the room, the result of a very empty stomach. "Not to worry, soon you will be fed, but first you will allow me to complete your examination. And I will inspect your rectum. I must know if the damage is inside of you or outside. Only then can I heal you. You will not fight me. Agreed?"

After a ten second pause, Philo realized the necessity. "I will not fight you."

"Wise decision. I saved you once. It is doubtful I can save you a second time."

"Artimos?"

"Yes."

"You will call me Philo."

"Agreed."

Philo's anger never waned, merely waited for good purpose. That would be in about six months, for that is the time necessary for an angry slave who has never held sword to become a skilled gladiator.

After the examination he was fed and bathed. I treated Philo's leather welts with a calming salve made from crushed leaves of the hibiscus. I gave Philo drink of an elixir (ingredients my secret, left behind in my journals for those who followed me) to speed the recovery of Philo's weakened condition from confinement to ship, whipping of his skin, punching of his belly and damage inflicted upon his rectum. The anal wound was internal. A tearing. It was not permanent, and I did not ask him how it came to be there. I tended to Philo the entire day, supervising Philo's full body massage given by strong-fingered male servants with first warm, and then cold palm oil.

I gave Philo hope and reason, for the life of a gladiator compared to most slaves is not such a bad thing, not until time comes for him to live or die in the arena. In between, Philo would be pampered as the valued commodity he was brought here to be.

He would grow strong, stronger than he already was. As this Macedonian approached his 21st year of life he stood naked at five feet and ten inches. His chest measured 39 inches but would expand to 41 before his trainer was satisfied. Short, dark hair covered his sternum and pectorals, forming a single line drawn from the pit of his stomach to his belly button, where below that his line of fur spread into a triangular wedge connecting to his pubic hair. His head covering was kept shaved to stubble of black with sporadic specks of bronze. His black brows enhanced beautiful cobalt eyes of blue. His upper torso's V shape melded flawlessly to his sturdy hips, while majestic curves defined his thighs, calves, biceps, triceps and forearms. Philo the Macedonian stood as a compact powerhouse, weakened on the day of his arrival, but more and more imposing with each passing hour in his Ludus Magnus home. The highlight of my week was to have him standing naked in my examination room for his measurements.

On two practice fields and with harmless weapons of wood, Philo was taught every aspect of every skill required to survive in the arena. His lanista, his instructor, one Argo Baltius, whose agent in Veneton made purchase of Philo on his behalf, also taught Philo proper etiquette to please the crowd and honor the sponsor of the games on any given day. Baltius was a good man compared to many lanistas. He instilled pride in the men he owned. They were made to feel as though an extension of him, and on the 168th day of training Argo proclaimed Philokrates of

Veneton Philo the gladiator. He was ready for the arena, next event.

What Philo did not learn was much of anything about any of the other men either in training or those maintaining their fight readiness for upcoming games. These men came from all over the Empire and spoke different tongues, but regardless, even those who could communicate were not allowed to do so. There were to be no friendships started nor enemies made, for each man was to internalize his thoughts to his one and only purpose: he belonged to the Emperor; he was to give all of himself to his Emperor. He would train to be the best, withstand whatever pain was necessary, and if need be, die in the effort. And to sanctify his commitment, he took the gladiatorial oath, which transformed his involuntary status of slave to voluntary status of gladiator: *I will endure to be burned, to be bound, to be beaten, and to be killed by the sword.*

Despite this oath, life for Philo in the Ludus Magnus was pleasant and fulfilling. At most he was to fight in the arena five times per year, and as I told him, the arena itself was Philo's only opportunity to end his bondage. In unambiguous Hellenic words spoken for Philo's precise understanding, I explained it all.

"You must always win, Philo, and you must do so with drama. The arena is theater. You must excite the crowd, and you must gain the Emperor's favor. Please him, and you become a hero. Heroes never die, Philo. Always remember this."

A Day for Vespasian

As was usual custom, the editor (producer/sponsor/scheduler) for this day's program threw Philo into a nearly hopeless situation. The good news? Philo would participate in the climax. The bad? Philo would face the most experienced and best skilled of all gladiators, a man named Ovid, a man who also happened to be the favorite of Emperor Quintillus.

The Emperor's reign approached its fifth month as the Amphitheatrum Flavium approached its 200th year. As for the overall history of the games -- mock animal hunts, festivals of gladiatorial contests, staged naval battles, chariot races and executions of violent criminals as public spectacle -- these had been ongoing for more than 800 years. In other words it was old news, but this day in A.D. 270 was of great significance. It commemorated not only the day of the Amphitheatrum's beginning but also the Emperor who ordered its construction in A.D. 70 -- Vespasian. His ascension to power marked the beginning of the Flavian line of rulers. Vespasian and his two sons in succession, Titus and Dometian, built the Amphitheatrum bearing their name.

Therefore, today's games were initially organized, planned and paid for by Emperor Claudius Gothicus himself, not from the governmental treasury, and even though the enthusiasm for such events under normal circumstances had waned, this was no ordinary celebration. The Colosseum was filled to capacity with 50,000 gathering to commemorate our Empire's glorious history.

To think that the entire event was nearly cancelled.

Long story in as few words as I can manage: Claudius II received title of Claudius Gothicus for his quelling of a Gothic invasion the early part of A.D. 270. Mostly taking place in Moesia, 50,000 were killed, some by Romans, some by plague. Unfortunately, this same plague also inflicted Claudius and he died from the disease. His brother Quintillus assumed the imperial throne only to be replaced by Aurelian, the general most influential in aiding Claudius with his successful campaign against the Goths. Mysteriously, Quintillus died about the same time Aurelian arrived in Rome September 270. Such was life and death at the top, but we commoners had grown accustomed to these power struggles. We merely wanted someone in place long enough so we could have our show. That turned out to be Aurelian, and so, the games were on. He finalized the preparations begun by the other two for Vespasian's glorious day, dedicating these games to Claudius Gothicus as well, but conveniently omitting Quintillus.

Because Philo's slot ended the day-long program, the wait for him was all day long. He and his opponent, Ovid, stayed behind in their Ludus Magnus cells, while the morning events in the Amphitheatrum started with a procession to honor the Flavians, followed by a staged animal hunt complete with living trees and green brush covering. All props rose from movable elevators beneath the arena's wooden-construct, sand-covered floor, and then trap doors in the floor opened to release African lions, Asian tigers and Germanic bears. Gladiators specially-trained for animal hunts called bestiarii entered the arena at floor level through the main opening near Aurelian's podium to seek their prey. More animals were killed than men, but that would change during the mid-day break for lunch.

As for me, I manned the triage set up a few yards inside the main stage entrance. Here I performed emergency treatments for those injured who had any chance for survival. Once finished with them I ordered servants cart them by stretcher through the tunnel back to the Ludus Magnus. If they still lived when the games were over and I could do more for them,

I did. As for those still living but mortally wounded, they were carted directly through the tunnel where servants trained by me gave them pain-killing elixirs back at the Ludus Magnus. And so, my morning was busy as injured beastiarii were brought to me incrementally, and it seems that no sooner had I finished with one than did another arrive. This is why I always looked forward to the individual gladiatorial contests when I could be more spectator than doctor.

During the break for lunch, some of those in attendance left the Amphitheatrum to purchase their meals from street vendors, while others stayed to watch continuing festivities. We staff (guards, lanistas and myself) stayed inside the staging areas where meals were provided.

As giant canvas awnings of ship-sail color were rolled out from the highest points of the Amphitheatrum's outer shell, shading spectators from an unusually warm autumnal day, lunch time brought executions of the condemned. These were serious criminals guilty of murder, arson, extortion or treason against the state. Murderers came first. They were tied by rope and crucified on classic crosses of patibulum and stipes, but their suffering was short-lived. Whatever animals survived the hunt still roamed the arena floor, and just in case the starving and frightened beasts weren't agitated enough, the bellies and legs of each crucified man were sliced open just enough to let blood. The excitement, of course, was watching and waiting to see which animal first discovered and was brave enough to try the available feast, and then the ensuing frenzy when all realized there was access to risk-free meat. After the predators ripped their victims down from the crosses and finished their easy-access meal, trap doors opened and bestiarii with whips and spears prodded and chased the belly-filled and more docile creatures back down to their cells beneath the arena floor.

Next came the remaining three groups of criminals, who were forced into the arena four at a time in order of the seriousness of crime. Each man was clad in loin cloth and on foot carrying short sword. Most were untrained for battle, but faced off two pairs of one against one in a fight to the death, and then those two winners faced each other until only one was left alive. That man remained to face a new opponent sent from the staging area, and if he survived that one he faced another until either all had been dispatched or exhaustion had caused his defeat. Whichever, the last man standing was granted a temporary reprieve from death with entry to the Ludus Magnus for training and future gladiatorial servitude.

With the Amphitheatrum seats once again filled by all spectators who had eaten out, the afternoon events began with a dramatic and slightly altered re-enactment of General Vespasian's quelling of a revolt in A.D. 67 which occurred in Judea. For this, jungle greenery was replaced by cliff rock and a replica of Jerusalem, and although in reality Vepasian returned to Rome before the city's siege actually took place, for us, gladiators representing him and his Roman legions defeated gladiators representing the Judeans in a nearly two-hour spectacle of clanking swords to shields and arrows to breast plates. Most deaths were feigned, but of course inevitably a few were genuine.

And so, as time drew near for the grand finale, Philo and Ovid were summoned for their long walk through underground tunnel to the Amphitheatrum. They were escorted by Roman Guard of the people, Tribunes. They strode single file, Ovid in front of Philo. Their wrists were bound by iron and chain same as their necks, a single neck-encircling chain connected from one man to the other. Once reaching the holding cells beneath the floor, their bindings were removed and they were outfitted for battle, soon to be given very real weapons to do very real battle.

Directly above them during this preparation, pairs of well-known and much-loved gladiators began their matches. These were the combatants considered to possess skills from good to very good, and each audience member had their favorites. Gladiators of grace and dramatic flair had their own groups of fanatics same as any athlete, and these fans placed wagers as eight men paired off one versus one. Each fought for victory. Each fought for cheers of approval, and by design the four pairs were spaced generously apart and near seating so that all fighters could be seen and enjoyed from any angle or distance.

With each pair refereed by lanistas from the Ludus Magnus, gladiators struck down and ready to concede defeat raised one index finger to the referee as his signal, but it was the crowd's decision as to whether the man's life was to be spared or taken. In each case the ultimate decision rested with Aurelian, but at this stage of the day's events it was rare for a man to suffer death in this manner, even if his wound was most likely to bring about his ultimate demise. The crowd had seen enough blood. This was a time to enjoy the glory of athletic competition and beauty of skilled gladiatorial performances. Granted, there would be men killed outright doing battle, but unless a fighter gave a lackluster performance, or if he'd lost several matches in succession and his fans were no longer willing to support him, a defeated gladiator could leave the arena to fight another day.

Not only did the Emperor schedule these pairings based on recommendations given him by their trainers, he also designated what type of gladiator they were to be, and each fighter's costume was designed to counter the protection worn by his opponent.

Thracian carried the heaviest equipment -- a helmet covering the entire head and grid visor for face; metal greaves from knees to ankles; small circular shield and short curved sword. The price for his protection and weaponry? He was made cumbersome, his movements restricted, and great stamina was required to carry such equipment during battle without becoming fatigued.

Secutor was armored but could move more easily -- an egg-shaped helmet covering face and head with two small and circular holes for eyesight; metal greave for but one leg; one arm protector for right arm made either of heavy fabric or leather; large rectangular legionnaire shield and long legionnaire straight sword. Other than more of his body being unprotected, his main disadvantage was limited vision through tiny eye holes. Because of his helmet's appearance he was called the fish, prey for the final gladiator on the list, the netter.

Retiarius had complete freedom of movement and vision -- no helmet or visor; one leather arm protector; one three-pronged trident; one rope-woven net and one small dagger. He needed to be quick and attack from angles, for other than loin cloth, sandals and arm protector his body was completely exposed.

There were variations on these themes, but most pairings involved one Retiarius, and the smart editor always chose men whose stature was short and stout to play this role -- men who were strong but not necessarily quick, of which Philo was one. Customarily and for good dramatic purpose, the favorite opponent of the Retiarius was the Secutor, and for this role men of slighter build and greater quickness were chosen, of which Ovid was one.

And so, with the final pair's match completed and a defeated man hearing merciful chants of mitte for "release him," Ovid and Philo stood inside shadows of the Emperor's entrance. Philo received his fishnet, as a Roman soldier draped it across his shoulder, threading its lassoed tether from the thumb to the wrist of his leather-protected left arm. Into his left hand was placed his dagger, into his right hand of bare arm went his trident, and Philo was ready for battle.

In a gallantly paced jog he entered twenty paces, his vision of dark shadow brightened by late afternoon sunshine, and for the first time Philo sensed the all-consuming energy of the Amphitheatrum Flavium. He was greeted warmly but not enthusiastically as he continued his proud gait to the one-third quadrant of arena floor. There, he stopped, turned and raised his trident in salute to Emperor Aurelian, who acknowledged Philo with palm facing him, fingers together and pointed to the heavens.

Proceeding in a knee-lifting strut to the center of the arena, Philo stood with trident raised, rotating his sandaled feet and fabric loin clothed hips to salute all in attendance, but by this time the crowd's polite hum had subsided to a murmur of anticipation.

They awaited their hero.

Ovid, affectionately nicknamed the Annihilator, his helmet secured between left arm and rib cage, shield in left hand and sword in right, cleverly angled his shield to reflect sun rays onto the crowd. His appearance to the majority a dazzling flash of light, Ovid majestically strolled to the one-third point of floor awash in a deafening roar of genuine admiration. Ovid, the Annihilator; Ovid, possessor of 22 wins, no defeats and 13 kills; Ovid, the favorite of our beloved but now dead Emperor Claudius Gothicus; Ovid, the favorite of our not-well-known but also now dead Emperor Quintillus, saluted his new Emperor Aurelian and basked in the worship of 50,000.

He stood bare-chested, shaven clean of hair to enhance muscle of chisel and sinew. He stood a fraction of an inch below six feet, sleek but powerful, an African leopard bred with African gazelle. He absorbed the energy of the crowd, saluted them where he stood, and channeled their adoration for him into an impenetrable confidence.

Ovid donned his helmet before proceeding to the center of the arena. With referee Argo Baltius in the far distance near a side wall and the crowd settling to a breath-held silence, Ovid peered through his tiny eye holes and spoke Roman tongue to his opponent.

"Prepare to die."

With a backhanded raising of right-handed sword, Ovid feigned a slash that instantly altered to a forward thrust, but unlike most netters Philo did not move back, did not believe the feint. Instead, he dipped his right shoulder and moved to the right, countering Ovid's forward thrust of not-there opponent with a downward flinging of his net. It wrapped Ovid's sword arm, but before Philo could yank free the sword, Ovid violently thrust his shield to the left, smashing Philo's face and chest. He stumbled backwards as Ovid unwound his net-bound arm with circular and counter-clockwise motion.

Both men stopped. Standing a distance of five feet apart, eyes met eye holes as Philo and Ovid analyzed their initial skirmish. A low-pitched buzz echoed the arena, the crowd also analyzing what they'd witnessed. This new fighter, this unknown force perhaps would not be so easily dispatched. They had expected the Annihilator to quickly annihilate, but now they sensed something far more dramatic and they shifted to the edge of their seats.

In Greek, Philo spoke his first words to the Secutor. "I will eat you, fish."

In Greek, Ovid replied. "My poison will kill you, netter." He raised his sword and charged. A mighty clanking of metal to metal greeted him, as Philo's horizontal trident held firm against Ovid's vertical sword.

"Your arm will break," said the fish in Greek.

"Then I will use the other," replied the netter in Greek, and he gave up resistance while moving to his right, leaving his right leg extended. Ovid lunged forward from the resistance not there and tumbled over Philo's leg, landing on his right and breaking his fall with right hand sword. Philo speared him from above, one prong of the three-pronged trident piercing Ovid's left flank just below his rib cage, the other two scraping his back, but as the net came down to capture the fish, Ovid gallantly rolled onto his back and with sweeping motion of sword caught the net before hacking into Philo's left ankle.

The impact partially slowed by net was not full force, but damage effective. Blood spilled, ligament was severed, and Philo howled while tumbling to land on his left side. As Philo dragged himself to a safer distance, Ovid let go his sword and shield. He rose to his feet, taking the still-imbedded trident with him. His roll onto his back to execute his sword strike forced the one prong of trident deeper into his flank, but still he was able to grasp it with both hands, yank it from his body and hurl it as far as his strength could muster, a tributary of blood flowing from his left flank into his leather loin wrap and re-emerging to paint his left leg. Seeing this, Philo scooted further away on his buttocks, and then struggled to regain his feet, standing on his right, dangling his left.

A deafening roar of standing approval enveloped the Amphitheatrum. The fish was speared, the netter crippled, but both men stood ready to continue their fight. New wagers were offered and given. Bettors hedged their Ovid bets with bets of rapidly-tightening odds for Philo, as the unknown fighter gained favor and respect.

The fish retrieved his sword and shield, but his left arm could not support the heavy metal length of shield, and so he dropped it, left it laying. The netter hopped on his right leg, dangled his left. With trident far from his reach he held net in left hand, dagger in right, and awaited Ovid's charge. It came quickly. Suspecting Philo unable to move left, the fish thrust forward to Philo's right. But Philo did move left. In a brilliant feat of dexterity he fell into a roll directed by his good right leg. The left side of his body tumbled leg to shoulder onto the floor, continuining until his right foot replanted with knee bent after his revolution. Philo's one good thigh and one good calf brought him standing a full three feet to the right of Ovid's air-piercing sword. Frustrated, Ovid repeated the move. Unfazed, Philo countered with another roll. A third attempt by the fish produced the same result, with audience wildly cheering each thrust of the fish and roll of the netter as though Ovid was the mighty bull seeking to gore Philo the elusive bullfighter.

A fourth thrust of the sword, however, was a feint. Ovid altered it to a slash. This time, Philo jumped back, the tip of sword catching his right hip on its downward movement. His fabric was severed, his skin opened, and Philo's loin cloth fell to reveal a minor flesh wound. With his dagger he caught the right arm of the fish as Ovid tried to pull his sword's tip out of the wooden floor. Philo's dagger pierced Ovid's arm protector, the blade imbedded to his forearm, gouging muscle, severing ligaments, and in response he let go his sword with right hand to smash the face of Philo with a left hand hook from his weakened left arm.

The netter fell onto his back, but not before grabbing the handle of Ovid's sword, removing it from the floor with his falling momentum and hurling it behind him as he fell. The fish stood with dagger protruding from his right forearm, and with what little grip from his left hand he could muster, Ovid removed the dagger, flinging it as far as he could opposite the direction of Philo's trident. He collapsed to his knees. Philo rolled onto his belly, rising to his knees and turning to face his opponent. They stared at one another four feet apart, their bodies drenched in sweat, painted with sand and blood.

No seat in the Amphitheatrum was occupied. Every Roman present including Emperor Aurelian stood silent, as did we, the staff. Everybody held breath in order to hear the breaths of two gladiators, their mighty chests heaving, their powerful bellies expanding and retracting. Shade covered these warriors, but not from awnings. Those had all been retracted, the sun having slipped beneath the western perimeter wall, leaving no more than a one-quarter sliver of light on the arena floor. By schedule and design, this match should have ended long ago. By now, Ovid should have taken his accolades and citizens taken their leave from the Amphitheatrum, but we Romans were unconcerned with this. Two heroes were doing battle. Two heroes were fighting with an intensity of evenly-matched skills rarely seen. Two heroes were giving their all and nobody had any intentions of going anywhere.

"From where do you swim, fish?"

"I come from Thebes. From where do you fish, fisherman?"

"Macedonia, fish. I believe the Romans envy us."

"True, fisherman. They wish to be Greek."

"We should honor them as they honor us."

"Fight like Greeks?" asked Ovid.

"Are we not Greek?" asked Philo.

"True. And we are without Roman weapons." Ovid looked beyond Philo's shoulder, saw his sword in the far distance. Philo looked left, saw his trident as a faraway stick. He turned right, saw his dagger as a speck.

"I have no strength to retrieve mine, fish."

"Your net is cut, netter."

"Useless. Join me, fish. Strip yourself naked. Let us enjoy what sunshine remains for us. We will fight as men, not fish and fisher."

"Agreed."

Both gladiators sat on their buttocks, removing their sandals, arm protectors and metal greave. As one they rose to their feet. Ovid lifted his helmet, exposing his wet-matted brownish-blond hair. He dropped his helmet. He dropped his leather loin cover, as Philo cast aside his tattered net. He accepted Ovid's offer of shoulder and neck, draping his arm across his opponent for support, and then, together, both men made their way for the narrow band of sunlight.

Argo, the referee, looked to his Emperor for guidance. Would such a violation of protocol be allowed?

Aurelian scanned his throngs of subjects, studying faces, listening for cries of protest. There were none. The arena was so quiet that the only sounds came from gladiator feet moving across arena floor sand. With a nod of his head, Emperor Aurelian approved.

The Amphitheatrum erupted as Ovid hobbled and Philo hopped, their manly sweat squishing between their naked bodies, and as they reached daylight two Greek warriors fought without weapon and without costume. They wrestled. They dealt and absorbed blows of forearms, kicks of feet, mixing their blood and their sweat with arena sand in a glorious display of masculine strength, perseverance and beauty. Ovid and Philo did battle for the Romans. They did battle for their Emperor, for the Flavians and Julio-Claudians and every line of Roman emperor since the Empire's birth. They battled for their Greek ancestors, their Greek gods and Greek mortals and Roman gods and Roman mortals. Ovid and Philo did battle until all of the Amphitheatrum was consumed by shadow and wonder and reverence for these two unyielding combatants, and neither Philo nor Ovid abandoned their battle until exhaustion, dehydration and loss of blood rendered them useless, until the entirety of them lay sacrificed to the arena floor.

"It is done, Ovid."

"Agreed, Philo."

And with both men sprawled on their backs gasping for air, two index fingers simultaneously pointed to the greying heavens, two naked warriors conceded their fates.

No Roman spoke. No Roman moved. Every Roman remained standing, listening, as two manly groans accompanied each exhale of breath. These sounds lifted from the arena floor to the seats and walls of the Amphitheatrum, through its arched entryways and into the streets of Rome. No witness to gallantry could approach this. No written or rumored accounts of bravery and sacrifice in the arena could compare, and the first word spoken by any Roman was not mitte, but liberare.

It started in the upper tiers amongst the plebeians. Within seconds it became a unifying chant in volume to crumble stone: **Liberare! Liberare! Liberare!**

Of course Aurelian would set them free. He would have done so regardless, but this historic moment had to be savored. He allowed the chant to continue, its volume increasing until eardrums ached. This was a good ache, a spirit-lifting ache. After all, the sole purpose of the games was to lift spirits, a time for an Emperor's subjects to temporarily forget their problems and their hatreds of one tribe or another and their discontent with him or his government or their tax burdens or any other wrongs trifling or serious they felt he'd brought upon them. Those citizens who'd witnessed this day's events would cherish these memories for the rest of their lives. Aurelian would forever value the performance given him by Ovid and Philo.

As Argo tended to Philo and Ovid's lanista tended to him, servants approached with water and stretchers. Aurelian raised his hand. The roar subsided, Amphitheatrum went quiet. Philo and Ovid drank, splashed their faces and rose to their feet. Refusing stretchers, they assisted one another in their long trek to the Emperor's podium. He stood above them by fifteen feet, his distance ten, his purple-trimmed toga wrinkled and tired from a very long day, and as Ovid and Philo stood with their fists raised in salute to him, Aurelian spoke.

"Gladiator Ovid, for nearly five years you have thrilled your Emperor and the citizens of Rome with your heroic exploits. Your skills are unmatched, and your performance today is deserving of the honor I am about to bestow upon you."

He tossed down to the arena a wooden sword. "I officially retire you undefeated from the Amphitheatrum Flavium." Next came a branch of the palm. "On this day I grant you your freedom." Then came handfuls of coins, gold coins, recently minted with Aurelian's likeness from the recently-disassembled and melted gold statue of the deposed and dead Quintillus. Ten hands were tossed, and finally, Aurelian hurled a laurel wreath. "I hereby declare you, Ovid, a citizen of Rome. May glory be with you and the Empire until the end of days."

A rare sight indeed, and those privileged to witness such an event erupted in celebration and approval. Ovid placed his wreath atop his head. He lifted his wooden sword in one hand, his palm branch in the other. He would acknowledge their appreciation and good tidings with a procession around the arena's perimeter. It was tradition. It was required, but Ovid would not move until his Emperor addressed his opponent, and with a raising of hand to quiet the crowd Aurelian did just that.

"Philokrates, it is with mixed emotions that I salute you. Today you fought your first battle in honor of Titus Flavius Vespasianus, in honor of Claudius Gothicus, in honor of Rome, and you did justice to all. You overwhelmed us with your courage, with your strength, and with your skills. You and Ovid gave us a performance unequaled in our history, and although my desire is to see you honor us with your bravery again and again, I cannot ask it of you. I will not have the possibility of your injury or death on my conscious. Therefore, Gladiator Philokrates," wooden sword was tossed, "I officially retire you undefeated from the Amphitheatrum Flavium." Palm branch was tossed. "On this day I declare you a free man." Five handfuls of gold coins and the laurel wreath were tossed. "I bestow upon you, Philokrates, full Roman citizenship and all privileges that come with it. May you live long and forever honor us as a fellow Roman."

Adrenaline alone propelled them. With wooden swords and palm branches in hands, laurel wreaths upon heads, both men made their way around the arena floor separate, but side by side. Philo planted his right foot and dragged his left while Ovid limped in favoring his right side over left side. They traversed near the wall but far enough away so that all could see. Rose petals were tossed. Perfumes and spices were tossed. Coins of all denominations were tossed, some striking the gallant men, but they felt nothing, for Ovid and Philo were elevated to a stimulating height no elixir can provide. The awe-inspiring outpouring of admiration and respect showered upon them eclipsed anything mortal men deserve to know, had a right to feel. They were oblivious to their tortured steps. Philo and Ovid floated on air in traversing the perimeter of arena floor.

And what happens to mighty warriors such as these when they finally make their exit from this theater, from this dramatic stage of unparalleled adoration? They collapse. They fall into a state of dreams, knowing that their fellow warriors will carry them to the healing space of their Ludus Magnus home, knowing that their fellow warriors will dutifully collect their riches from the arena floor because no man would dare steal from a hero. Philo and Ovid peacefully slept, knowing that their fellow Roman citizens would hail them as heroes until the end of their days.

Mine for Now

Cool air, soft light and contentment guided Philo from the depths of his sleep. The in between, the beginning of full consciousness is almost always pleasant, but for Philo this particular instance must have been exceedingly so.

His eyes opened to the color of pale grey, not the cold and dark of his cell. To his right was open window, a fresh breeze billowing sheer drapery. The sky was dark and with stars, but lights of the city brightened its hue to a calming purple. He laid not on a straw-stuffed mattress, but something soft, something that caressed every curve of his spine, buttocks and legs, and beneath his head was something even softer, something he'd only seen but never felt.

Philo laid on an actual bed -- my bed in my home, with pillows and soft linens to soothe him. Standing as a darkened silhouette a few paces to his left, I watched over his naked, fresh-skinned and pleasant-smelling body.

"Ah, I see you've decided to rejoin the living," I spoke in Roman tongue. He instantly recognized his physician's voice.

"Artimos? Am I truly with the living?"

"Very much so."

"How many days have I slept?"

"Two days, three nights." He tried to sit up, but was gently guided back down to the mattress by physician's hand to patient's shoulder.

"Artimos, what is this place?"

"This is my home, Philo. You were brought here late today."

"And Ovid? Is he here?"

"No. He remains at the Ludus Magnus."

"Will he..."

"He is not good, Philo. It will take more time for him."

Philo turned his head away, sucking life from the room to render it cold and silent. Such a mood could not be allowed and so I strolled into near darkness, returning with a bowl that reflected window light as though it were silver. It was silver, its diameter ten inches, depth six.

"Feel inside, Philo." He reached up to feel and hear the clanking of coins. "You have wealth, my friend... Roman wealth. When daylight comes you can count what is here."

"With your help."

Setting his bowl of coins to the floor, I helped him sit up with pillow between his back and the wall. "I brought you food and drink."

Atop bedside table sat a tray of foodstuffs and beverage which I had earlier prepared, but as I reached for it Philo's memory of a sword hacking his ankle caused him to lift his leg for inspection.

"Where's my..." he couldn't feel his foot but saw the shape of it matching his right. "Oh, good, I thought I might have... you saved my leg?"

"You were fortunate. Now, eat, drink... let me talk."

With tray on his lap, Philo dined from a platter filled with meats, cheeses, grapes and bread. He ate slowly, listened intently, as I explained matter-of-factly while sitting on the mattress beside Philo's left knee.

"The blade cut just above your ankle. It severed a ligament, some muscle. It chipped a bit of bone on your leg. I reconnected the ligament... stitched muscle, sewed your skin together. Then, we bathed you and let you be. You slept through all of it, but of course I helped with that."

"One of your elixirs?"

"Ha. Extract of the poppy while I worked on you. Then, the elixir." I took a deep breath to carefully construct my words, and then I spoke them. "Philo, your ligament will heal, but part of it could not be saved. The lost section is replaced by metal tube." Holding up my thumb and index finger, I gauged the tube's length for him to see. "Your ligament will not function below the tube, from ankle to foot. Your ankle will not rotate like before. Your foot will hang freely. You will have no movement there. You will walk with a limp. You will use a walking stick. You will..."

"Artimos?"

"Yes?"

Philo chewed and swallowed before continuing. "You speak as though it is written in stone."

"It is."

"It is not. You don't know me."

I looked for something to touch, some part of my naked patient's body that would convey compassion and perhaps a bit more. His left pectoral would do, the palm of my hand just above his nipple. "I want to know, Philo. Tell me."

"I will walk as a whole man."

"You believe this?"

"I know this."

"I have never seen it."

"You say all is connected?"

"Yes, but with metal tubing... and the length..."

"Then I will teach it to work. I will teach good ligaments to work for the bad."

Despite what medical knowledge tells me, I could not doubt Philo's words. My opinion is that the concept of mind over matter is a very real thing, and I knew that if it could be done, if any man could write a new text to the book of medicine, Philo was such a man. Philo possessed the strength of will necessary to do exactly what he said he would do.

"There are treatments that might help, Philo... exercises. I will show them to you, assist you with pain, but you must do the work."

"As you know I will." Philo placed his right hand atop my touching-his-pectoral hand. "Do you think I failed to notice your interest in me? How you have cared for me since my arrival?" He moved our hands in unison, bringing my underneath palm onto his nipple. "From the day I was beaten with leather and fists until right here and now, you have always tended to me before you did all the others... gave to me knowledge and hope. Helped me with the Roman tongue. Now you have kept me intact. Would it not have been easier to simply hack off my foot and be done with it? No, not for you. You kept my body together. You have given me a chance to remain a whole man. I owe you much, Artimos."

"You listened well, Philo. And now you are a freedman. It is everything I had hoped."

"Take my tray."

I returned it to the table.

"Your bed comforts me, Artimos. It is a pleasure I've never known." Philo maneuvered himself to lay flat. "Just think of it... I can do as I please... free to choose." He spread his arms to stretch. He yawned. "Mmm, Artimos, I feel as though the weight of a thousand stones have been lifted from me." Stretch finished, yawn finished, he left his arms so that each wrist touched mattress corner. Philo laid in a four-corner sprawl, naked upon my mattress.

What I did, I did in actions, not words. Methodically, gently, I reaped my reward for seven months of patience and restraint. From day one my self-control was proper and admirable. I stopped myself from intervention as Roman leather wailed upon Philo's beautiful Macedonian skin, whereas without restraint I would have run to my tortured hero and licked every wound clean while taking the leather blows myself. Without restraint, I could never have stood there watching Drusus Macarius pulverize Philo's gloriously sculptured belly to a pulp. I could never have remained idly listening to the defiant groans and grunts that accompanied each impact of powerful fist to his brick wall. Without restraint, I would have chased Drusus and his partner away, run to my suffering Philo, wrapped my arms around Philo and buried my face into Philo's belly, and I would have suffocated myself before ever letting go of him.

Now I could. My servants were day servants, gone for the evening. The house was ours. Philo rested. I joined him in nakedness, and I worshiped him.

I knelt beside his massive chest, lowering my cheek into its fur covering.

I breathed in his fresh aroma, tickled my nose with his chest hairs. My lips touched him here, planting kisses onto the length of his sternum. I explored either side of it, pressing my lips deep into his pectoral muscle. Stumbling upon a dime-sized nipple, nearly hidden and pointing down when its owner stood but now stretched wide open and in my full view, I opened my lips to surround it. With my tongue I tasted his handsome orb, feeling its diameter shrink and tip rise from my warm and wet stimulation. Both nipples were praised before I left them glistening and moved from his rib cage to his stomach, from hard bone to hard muscle.

I did bury my face into that belly, but lightly, because an erect penis covered a good portion of its surface. Philo didn't know the difference between the touch of a female and touch of a man. Neither had ever touched him for any purpose other than to work knots out of his sore muscles, or to punish him, and so Philo responded as any man responds to affection. He basked in the praise heaped upon him. He was a freedman, a grown man, free to allow the only person who'd ever shown him affection of any kind show him the most meaningful affection of all -- the affection of friendship, of admiration and of trust.

Philo, a novice, could not have known that his physician had other skills besides that of surgeon, dietitian, strength-builder and health-maintainer. Only through experience with others could he know that the ability to engulf both penis and testicles into one's mouth is a rare gift. I speak as though an expert, which is false, for not even I knew such skills were in my possession, not until the penis and testicles in question were those belonging to Philo. I could and did. Kneeling between Philo's thighs, I took his engorged phallus to the back of my throat, extended my tongue to lift his gonads, and closed the gap beneath them with my lower lip.

Size was not an issue, neither a help nor a hindrance, for this man's genitals were perfectly proportioned to his five-ten frame. His erect penis covered two-thirds of the space between pelvis and navel, its thickness powerful like its owner. The roundness of his tight-skinned testicles plump and prime, they were identically shaped and separated by high ridge of skin. Desire spurred me to achieve my goal. For so long had I waited, hoping but not expecting to ever have this man right here surrendered in my bed. What were the odds that Philo would leave the Ludus Magnus alive? Not just on the day for Vespasian, but on any day ever after? Slim to none. But now, not only was Philo a freedman, he also was free to give himself to my care as his physician and beyond. My dreams had come true very quickly, and I endeavored to show Philo that this was his new home, that never again would he need to look elsewhere for his comfort.

With his first explosion wholly consumed I laid on my side next to Philo's chest, his right arm wrapping my shoulder, his left arm moving from mattress corner to between his head and pillow. His right pectoral was my pillow, and I listened to his breathing slowly return to normal pace. With his body he thanked me. His muscles, although naturally hard, relaxed. Philo was at ease, totally comfortable with me, and if I had any lingering doubts as to his acceptance of all that had transpired to this point, Philo erased them with talk. For once, I listened.

He told of his father's conscription to the legions when he was but four years old, of how upon his father's death his mother went through father's wages and death benefit in less than one year, and of how she gave him up at age five to the care of a Macedonian consulate who reported to Roman governor. Philo grew up on an estate outside the Veneton city walls, worked as servant in the fields and orchards, tended to horses in the stables. And although the consulate never mistreated him, the food rations given him as a five year old never increased as he grew older, and the hunger never left him. For years he sneaked food when possible until he was caught and he was prosecuted.

Although a prisoner, his construction work built a strong body and sharp mind. He mixed the lime, water and volcanic ash used as mortar to build aqueducts. He laid that mortar and assisted in guiding the cut stones from scaffold suspension and pulley ropes onto the previous layer. Philo considered himself lucky in that most men of this profession lost fingers, thumbs, hands or entire limbs from the falling too soon or falling out of position stones that weighed tons. Perhaps he was lucky, perhaps smart, but either way everything changed when a Roman crew chief took a liking to him. And since Philo had no intention of succumbing to this man's wishes regardless of Philo's prisoner status, the man proceeded to take what he wanted, enlisting three others to assist him. Four times was Philo violated, his feet in leg irons, face pressed into dirt and arms held down by the others as each took his turn.

The charge of attempted escape was necessary to counter Philo's complaint to the lead engineer on their project. His humiliation of standing naked on the auction block with dried blood clearly visible on his inner thighs -- those same stains five days later still visible enough to draw my attention, which instigated my attempted inspection that would bring him further punishment from the fists of Drusus to his gut -- only intensified Philo's hatred of all Romans.

Thanks in part to my advice on how best to use it, Philo's hatred served him well, brought him success beyond his wildest hopes, and as Philo summed up his life for me our bonds strengthened. We trusted. With my head resting on Philo's right breast, my hand gently rubbing his left breast, I absorbed everything he said without interrupting him -- no questions, no requests to fill in gaps, no patronizing expressions of sorrow -- because I wanted him to get through it. Philo needed to be done with it. We both did.

When the last word was spoken, when Philo went silent except for his heavy, catching up breath from his lengthy summary, I continued my silence, putting my mouth to better use by extracting a second dose of Philo's seed.

Sunrise would begin new journeys for both of us, but for now I brought an empty bowl and placed it between his thighs, draping his spent penis over its rim for him to urinate. I dumped it in the commode, masturbated while I was there and returned to my position of head on Philo's chest.

For closure, and to make certain he knew I was content and expected nothing more from him, I officially ended our first night together.

"You're a survivor, Philo." I pecked his nipple with my lips. "Nothing can defeat you, and I am honored to have you in my home for as long as you wish."

A Boner Book

Persephone's Second Fidget

A rather exhausting schedule awaited. Days found me at my paid position tending to gladiators in the Ludus Magnus, and here my main concern was with Ovid. Much like Philo's leg, Ovid's forearm required surgery to stitch damaged muscle and reconnect ligaments. Ovid lost more blood in the arena than did Philo, and worse yet, his liver was slightly punctured. Yellow bile circulated his bloodstream, and although the liver would heal itself with time, bile is poison and Ovid's body temperature elevated.

He carried fever that would not break and for remedy I kept him constantly warm, ordering servants to wrap him in hot-water-soaked linens on the hour every hour. To assist Ovid's body in filtering out the bad blood, I drained from him one pint each day. No other treatments were known, and so this was the everyday routine. I watched and I waited.

Adding to the solemn mood awaiting me at work each day, Drusus Macarius came in early to catch me on his last day.

"I've joined the city battalions, Artimos. Filed for election to Tribune."

"Way to go, my friend. Do you know where you will be stationed?"

"Not yet. After tonight's shift, I have one week to idle before reporting to command."

"Well, Drusus, I'm happy for you, but sad for us."

"I need fresh air, Artimos."

"Remember that you said that when winter comes, when you're standing inactive freezing your ass."

"Take the good with the bad, right Artimos?"

And Drusus was right. My current bad was Ovid, but this was countered by Philo. My nights were with him. He spent his days mostly resting and saving his strength for evening. My good old maidservant Brusilla, a woman of 50-some-odd years who came from Gaul, a woman who for the past twelve of those years had faithfully kept the underling servants in line while keeping me properly fed in a house spotlessly clean, did most of what was needed in tending to Philo during the day. She never saw his addition as being an unfair burden upon her. She favored the new spirit he brought to both the household and its master. She washed Philo, brought him meals and bedpans so that by the time I arrived home Philo was ready for his therapy.

My house stood two stories tall, four street crossings from the Amphitheatrum. It was built more than one hundred years prior for physicians like myself assigned to the Ludus Magnus. It was government-owned, its outside appearance humble but interiors spacious, its rectangular shape constructed of neatly cut, stacked and mortared stone. The floors and ceilings were surfaced with panels of pine. It was surrounded on three sides by privately-owned houses of same construct but of only one story heights. The land upon which it sat once had been an open-air garden, part of an estate dating to days of the Republic before there were any Emperors. On street level was my kitchen, bath, commode, and one spacious open area partitioned for dining and for relaxing. The upstairs was one room containing my bed, a combination shelf and desk area for my library, one large closet for my clothes and a larger one for storage.

This second story gave us privacy, and until Philo could navigate stairs this was where he always stayed. His therapy began with walking. Just as Ovid had done in the arena, I assisted him with my shoulder. This allowed Philo to add weight to his steps in increments of his choosing, guided by warnings from me against doing too much too quickly. Stretching exercises were done in the form of lunges when standing, my hands holding his for support in front of him.

Everything else took place upon the bed mattress. With Philo on his back, I raised his left leg to vertical and manipulated Philo's foot with my hands.

Artimos?

Yes, Philo.

Persephone fidgets, and so do I.

My syrup is too thick?

Your history is precise and details thorough, but now we must get to the point in order to make the point. Besides, I don't talk like that. My speech is vulgar at times. You have said so yourself.

I will have you no other way.

In that case, you rest, I'll talk.

Artimos pushed me to my limits, but he also rewarded me at session's end with deep-fingered, palm-oil lubricated rubbing to my arms, back and legs, which led to him rolling me over so he could suck me dry. Do you suppose I could ever leave him? Even if I could walk by myself? This was our routine every night for nearly three weeks until he came home with a walking stick for me, claiming that his shoulder was worn out from supporting me. Liar.

It was a handsome little tool made of sturdy oak, its handle seven inches so that I could control it with fist forward or fist to the side. Its foot was flat surface squared three inches and covered with roughed-out rhinoceros hide to give me grip. Artimos made purchase of my stick for good price, for he and the woodcraftsman were well-acquainted from the many canes, crutches and special splints needed for crippled and healing gladiators. There was none like it in all of Rome. Artimos gave it to me so that I could negotiate stairs, and my training began right then and there in our home with Artimos staying in front of me in case I stumbled.

I could be an arrogant ass. I could tell you that my own strength and perserverence made my ankle work again, but that would only be half true. This was a team effort. Artimos restored me, not merely from the physical hacking of my leg, but also from the mental hacking of my spirit. Aurelian granted me my legal freedom; Artimos gave me the confidence and knowledge to enjoy it.

From that time forward, our nightly sessions ended with mutual admiration. No matter that my ankle ached and throbbed from its workout, I felt no pain when taking hold of his ankles to drape his legs over my shoulders. Palm oil makes for easy entry. Artimos will modestly say that he is nothing but a 42 year old balding softie, but he lies. Artimos is strong as can be when he puts out the effort, and when my dick is in his ass he crushes me down to nothing. As though his oral talents weren't enough to keep me around, his rectal skills can get me to blow loads back to back -- sometimes three times if the planets are aligned properly.

And so I'm sure you understand why, walking stick or no, I never considered striking out on my own. Artimos and I were set financially and emotionally. We had all we needed. Even made plans for his future retirement from the Ludus Magnus, discussing nightly which ocean side towns in the Empire might be suitable for our growing-old-together villa.

This might have been our happy ending had Ovid not spoiled everything. None of it was his fault. Unconscious for three weeks, when Ovid finally came out of it the wolves were waiting. Well, one wolf -- Tacitus Galeo, one of the wealthiest grain brokers in all the Empire. The only thing fatter than his pockets was his oversized gut. He's a meddler and image was everything to him. So, naturally, he wanted Ovid as an employee. Everyday he dropped in to ask Artimos about his patient, and when Ovid finally came out of it Galeo was right there to tempt him with riches. Ovid didn't need Galeo's money. His take from the arena floor was greater than mine, but like me, Ovid knew nothing about being a freedman nor the dangers that come with it. This is why we wanted Ovid with us, at least temporarily until he could decide the best way to go with the rest of his life. Specifically, I felt an obligation to him. Without Ovid, my good fortune could never have come the way it did. I considered him my spiritual brother. We both were slaves brought together for purpose. Now we both were freedmen and should be together again.

Besides all of this, Artimos suspected Ovid's brain might be damaged from his poisoned blood and many days of coma, and Artimos did everything in his power to keep Ovid there under his protection until he could be sure of Ovid's stability. But men like Tacitus Galeo stop at nothing to get what they want. He went over the doctor's head, threatening the administrator of the Ludus Magnus with impressive arguments of his supposed good standing with our new Emperor Aurelian, plus a long list of powerful men who could crush a minor paper pusher with the snap of their fingers.

And so, Ovid was released from the care of Artimos and his downward spiral began. He became body guard for Galeo, health and fitness trainer to Galeo's wife, Livilla, and the wives of Galeo's circle of friends. That was his day job. For his nights, Ovid discovered that liquid spirits masked his pain, namely, Tuscan wine and Egyptian beer. He frequented the lowliest of wine and dines, bedding any prostitute smart enough to take him home. Smart because Ovid had no sense of money management. He carried large sums with him but always awoke with none. It should have come as no surprise that he also bedded his daytime women, all of whom happened to be married. And it certainly was no surprise when Galeo sent an assassin with purpose of catching Livilla and Ovid in the screwing process.

This is when, finally, after five months of hell-raising, Ovid came to visit me. By this time I was nearly self-sufficient, needing my walking stick only for stairs. That was physical. As for smarts, Artimos had taught me many things regarding Roman society and how it works, but I still had a long way to go and was about to make a serious blunder.

Ovid arrived during the afternoon, his clothing stained in blood. The eyes of Galeo's wife alerted him that a dagger was about to be plunged into his back, at which time he quickly rolled off the top of her so she could take the dagger to her lung. He wrestled with the man Galeo sent to kill him, secured the dagger for himself and gutted the assassin.

Brusilla, Artimos's long-time maidservant gave Ovid fresh clothes while I got him some money for travel. Half hour after he left our house a group of men arrived to take me away and at this point I get so angry I could spit. Artimos, I can't tell the next part without sounding arrogant, and besides, I'm out of breath. Please take over and you can mush it up to your heart's content.

Don't worry, Philo. I will.

Ostia Harbor

My maidservant Brusilla knew Philo was in serious danger, and she prevented our bad situation from becoming disastrous. Upon Ovid's exit from our house, Brusilla sent the underling servants back to their homes. Next, she burned Ovid's bloody clothes in the kitchen fire, destroying them completely just before men burst through the front door. She hid in a kitchen nook. They never entered the kitchen, some went upstairs making much noise, others stayed downstairs making more, and then they all left taking Philo with them. That's when she came running to me at my workplace, telling me all that had happened.

I kissed her forehead. "Brusilla, you are a cherished friend." She received my pouch containing every coin I had on me. "Take this. Leave the city. You are now a freedwoman. Return to your homeland."

She bowed her head, thanked me for my kindness to her during her years of service, took her money and ran like hell, for she knew as well as I that household servants are put to torture when incidents such as this occur. Here we had a case of adultery and a double murder with the suspect undoubtedly seen entering and leaving our house, which made it most likely Praetorian guards had arrested Philo.

However, Brusilla never saw the men who took Philo. What if Tacitus Galeo decided to take matters under his own control? Before the local magistrate had received word of the incident and processed the necessary paperwork for an official arrest? Either way, I prepared myself to do battle with one or the other, and then spoke with my adminstrator about my need to leave for the day. He was told the truth. Ovid was on the run, may or may not have murdered Livilla Galeo, and Philo would need me there when and if the authorities questioned him.

"He is not aware of legalities," I explained. "He does not understand that he has implicated himself."

My boss, who already was sickened by his being forced to release Ovid from my care in the first place, had no desire of adding Philo to his list of failures. He granted my request.

My arrival home found the house ransacked. Our readily-available spending coins were gone, but our fortune-building coins remained safely intact in our three separate hiding places. That answered the question of which entity had taken Philo. Thievery, destroying property, abduction of a freedman, Tacitus Galeo oozed of slime, and Philo's earlier description of him does us all a disservice.

Tacitus married wealth and used it to build his empire, multiplying his wife's investment tenfold. I'm certain that at one time he was a handsome man, but these days he sported a grotesquely extended belly and two unsightly warts upon his crooked face -- one to the left of his nose; one to the right of his lower lip. He was an expert on everything from wine to gladiators, or so he would have you believe. His long-winded diatribes peppered with expensively unnecessary words meant to impress could drive one to distraction, force his listener to seek an escape route. As for gladiators, he secretly owned many through his agent and trainer Macro Callistus. Philo was never his. Ovid was. And I'm quite certain his coercing Ovid into his employment had more to do with his lost property than with his interest in Ovid's welfare. Owners of gladiators freed by Emperors are not compensated for their loss. It is considered a gift to Rome from a wealthy slave owner with no appeals heard.

Upon his marriage to Livilla, he set about to corner the grain markets, enlisting the aid of street bullies to intimidate smaller merchants into "merging" with his company. Those who refused seemed to mysteriously disappear for a few days before returning to announce their new partnership. Behind his back the elite joked of him, but to his face they showered him with praise for his many accomplishments and knowledge. The Imperialii tolerated him because for better or worse his tactics in Rome and his many connections throughout the Empire kept the grain bins full and prices fair, and I'm quite sure by now you have guessed that my lengthy description of him means that he would be a dangerous adversary. It should also be clear that it was his men who eventually arrived to take me away. Good. If I couldn't locate Philo, how could I help Philo?

"You are Artimos? The Greek doctor?" Asked their apparent leader.

"Yes."

"I am Timor. Tacitus Galeo asks that you visit with him. You will come with us."

Well, that wasn't really asking now, was it? First, they searched me, finding nothing, and then they stuffed me into Livilla Galeo's carpentum. This is a wooden wagon with metal carriage on top used by the pompous to displace street pedestrians so they can pass unseen. Only important people could legally use such an item on crowded Roman streets during the daytime. With its back door shut, the carriage is completely enclosed except for open slits near its top for ventilation of air, slits through which passengers could peer out but gawkers could not peek in.

Tacitus sent five men to abduct me. Imagine that! Five dagger-weilding brutes required to take away a little old harmless doctor such as myself. Three joined me inside, two rode atop, one to guard, one to drive the single horse. The afternoon was late on an unusually warm May day, and by the time we exited the city walls and traversed 18 miles to the Ostia Harbor a mere sliver of the sun remained hovering above the ocean.

The dock and warehouse workers were changing shifts. Day workers

A Boner Book

who offloaded ships for storage in warehouses gave way to night workers who distributed goods onto barges for delivery via the Tiber into the city at sunrise, and amidst the rows of one-story warehouses one building dominated all the others. Solidly constructed of heavy cut stones stacked and mortared, its color darkened grey from countless decades of silt-laden harbor winds, this two-story monstrosity commanded warehouse row as if a fortress standing watch.

Cut into the stone archway above its entry doors were letters indicating this building as the Ostia Grain Exchange, where merchants once bartered with shipping agents to lock in future prices for future shipments, a function long ago abandoned and dating back to the days of the Republic.

The inside was more desolate than the out. An opening of front door brought clicking sounds of scurrying rat's feet, leaving nothing on the wooden floor but a few scattered writing tablets separating dust from wood. All fixtures were stripped, the windowless walls bare except for the very back wall where one door stood open with beam of light glowing. Single file we walked, two thugs in front of me, three behind, and in passing through the doorway I saw to my right an open trap door making a square hole in the floor, while to my left was a solid block of wood with lit candle, flanked by one empty chair and one occupied chair.

"Good to see you, Artimos. Come, take a seat."

Tacitus Galeo dressed comfortably for this occasion -- single-piece brown wool tunic stopping above his more-meat-than-bone knees and strap sandals on his extremely-wide feet. He slouched in his chair with fingers locked together and resting on his ball-shaped belly, thumbs tapping his fabric as I accepted his invitation to sit.

"Shouldn't you be home remembering your wife, Tacitus?"

"Men deal with grief in their own way. I will be interested to see how

58

you handle your grief."

"For what? Did somebody else die?"

"Don't be coy, Artimos. You know who."

"Ah, Philo. I wondered why he was not at home. Is he here, too?"

"He most certainly is. Came to pay us a visit. We've done some preliminaries on him, but as you might suspect I have yet to learn anything of interest."

"Hmm... so, let me ask you this. Have you now expanded your business enterprises to include abduction?"

Apparently, Galeo did not find my attitude proper because he violently stood with a force to send his chair tumbling backwards.

"Listen here, doctor," he scolded me with pointing of his fat finger. "My Livilla was murdered today. The perpetrator of this foul, heinous, unwarranted execution of treachery is an entity well-known to you, to me, and to every Praetor, Magistrate, Consul, Senator, patrician citizen, plebeian citizen, even our glorious Emperor Aurelian himself. We all know who did this to my beloved soulmate, my precious, angelic, purely innocent reason for life itself, and the instigator was last seen leaving your house. Philo assisted him. Philo is well-aware of his whereabouts. That is called harboring a fugitive from justice, my friend, aiding and abetting, circumventing what is right and good and fair to those who obey the law, to those who respect the law, to those who tremble beneath the solid principles upon which this magnificent Empire was constructed."

See? I told you about him. Good god almighty, what a windbag! Such drama!

Remaining seated and peaceful, I politely countered his accusations. "Excuse me, but I believe these are things for a magistrate to hear. Or have you appointed yourself as such? What I do know is that Philo is a freedman. Have you forgotten this? Perhaps our new Emperor will be interested to know that you hold prisoner a man he himself declared a Roman citizen. As far as that goes, I am the same. You have no right to hold either one of us here. Do the Imperial codes mean nothing to you? Think of your reputation."

"Don't concern yourself with my reputation, you Greek shit. If things go as I plan there will be no tongues remaining to speak of my reputation."

And with that (thank heavens) pointed response, I was persuaded to join the single file line moving to the trap door, where waited a stairwell of single person width. Thug numbers one and two descended in front of me, followed by Galeo, Timor and thugs four and five.

That last comment of his did not bode well for us, but I hoped it was said for purpose of intimidation rather than fact. Tacitus, unlike myself, was well-versed in these types of contests. Many Romans, especially those from the old-time patrician family lines played such games on a regular basis and had done so for centuries. As for me, I always tried my best to keep my eyes, nose, mouth and ears out of such matters, but this time I had no choice. My intent was to keep my wits, to present a facade of calm, and to not let anger choose my words. Make no mistake, this game was deadly serious. If you don't believe me, just ask the Julio-Claudians -- oh, I'm sorry, you can't. For decades they secretly poisoned or openly tortured and murdered one another in their zeal to become the next Emperor, until the day Nero ordered his servant to gut him before the Senate could declare him an enemy of the state. When he died, not one man with one drop of Julio-Claudian blood in his veins was left to take the throne.

As my head cleared the floor that became the ceiling, I was presented with the man I'd hoped to find -- Philo, atop a round table, stripped naked, glistening with sweat, ankles and wrists bound with rope, arms and legs stretched and quartered to form the letter X.

I hesitated four steps from the final step as the two in front of me cleared the way. Philo's feet were closest to me, his gloriously handsome feet, their soles masculine and white, arches sturdy and strong. The thickness of his calves and thighs became even more grand with their flattening to the table. His mighty chest rose high, which caused his belly to slope towards me, and as he lifted his head to inspect who was taking so long to descend the stairs, those abdominal muscles came to life, a deep ridge drawing a line straight to his navel and below, flared curves in pairs numbering three extending from either side of the ridge. He locked eyes with mine, hinted a smile and strained against his ropes to display himself. Did he do this for me? Damned right he did. My motivation.

Only a few seconds were given for me to enjoy his performance, because with a sinister, "get moving," Tacitus shoved me tumbling down the remaining steps. I landed on my chest, breaking my fall with hands, and under the table was a stick broken into three pieces -- Philo's walking stick, made for and gifted to a crippled gladiator, now rendered useless. Seems Galeo's admiration and respect for warriors of the arena was nothing more than boastfully hot air.

Hot air partially describes the atmosphere of this underground room, but stifling is more apt. Stale, heavy and unmoving also describes it. After waiting for Galeo, Timor and the other two to step over and past me, I scrambled to my feet and moved towards Philo, but was redirected by the hand of Timor, who clutched my arm and yanked me towards one of two wooden stools. Their seats round and without backing, their legs stood fifteen inches and they flanked a square table. Sitting atop the table was a water-filled bucket and behind the table sat a wooden barrel filled with much more water.

Tacitus sat to my left, while my stool position aligned me with Philo's right hip, his distance from me four feet. Beyond him about six feet from his left, two wall-mounted brackets held two torches lit to illuminate both Philo and enough of the room to show me we were in open space, the basement of the building running its full length and width. Beyond Philo's head sat another square table with tools on top, their distance too far for me to define them.

"He is quite a speciment," Tacitus observed while his men taunted Philo, surrounding the table to poke and prod him with their bony fingers.

"He's an athlete. A gladiator. Remember? You should respect that, rather than destroy it."

Oh, don't worry. None of my tortures will mutilate."

"Small comfort that is. After the performance he and Ovid gave you in the arena, one might think we could honor them by handling this in a more civlized manner."

"Their performance insulted me... insulted the gods. How dare they remove their battle armaments. How dare they strip naked and wrestle like heathens. There is nothing civilized about either one of them. No honor."

Since Tacitus gave me no quarter with my respect for gladiators angle, and Philo gave Tacitus no indication that the torment of brutes effected him, I asked a very important question.

"Tacitus, are there facilities in this building?"

"No. Why? Do you need to piss?"

"Worse. The porridge I had for lunch is finished with me."

"Pity you. There's a commode hole back there." He pointed over his left shoulder. "No water. It was diverted long ago. No sponges, no stick. You'll have to wipe with whatever you can find."

"Let's pray for a clean break."

"You pray. It is your problem."

The tiny room was barely visible, two partitions extending from the outer wall perpendicular to the torch-bearing wall. Along the way I spied two chains dangling from the ceiling with wrist-cuffs attached, and then I stubbed my toe on a wooden t cross laying on the floor. Galeo's torture chamber seemed well equipped and I shuddered to think Philo might visit all three of his devices. For that matter, I myself might feel what they could do. At this point the only positive development I could observe was that when busy in his dungeon Galeo's words tended to be more direct. Praise heaven! Any more of his long-winded speeches down here and we could all suffocate.

Whatever feces couldn't be transferred from fingers to partition was smeared on my clothing. With all the other foul smells in this dank basement, a little shit would make little difference.

"Success?"

"I've had worse." With Philo not yet feeling pain, only frustration, I allowed myself to admire the dramatic image he presented. His masculine form barely reacted to the tauntings of five men surrounding the table. They too were uncomfortable with this stagnant air, and had during my visit to the commode removed their clothing down to fabric loin cloths. Brutish men they were, not far removed from imported apes seen in the arena. Short in height, their jowls extended beyond their foreheads. Their chests were thick and heavy with scant tapering of flank between rib cage and pelvic bone. Timor and one other were covered with black, animal-like hair front and back from head to toe, while the others were lightly carpeted, also with fur of black. They smelled of many days's sweat. A new layer glistened their skin, matted their fur, dripped from their foreheads, streamed in tributaries from their arm pits down their ribs and made them smell even worse. I pitied Philo for having to be so near them.

From all directions their fingers poked his ribs, poked his stomach, poked his thighs, calves and soles of feet. They tugged his body hairs anywhere and everywhere, pinched his skin for brief seconds between fingers and thumbs. He never flinched, never uttered protests. Preliminary, that's all this was. Philo knew it. His serious torture was still to come, and yet he showed no fear, only disgust. He raised his head with a smirk, watched them work him over, and then sighed heavily as though bored before returning his head to the table.

"Your boy seems to think he has nothing to fear from me," said Galeo.

"I see no boys here. I see two innocent men and six criminals."

"Well, perhaps this will open your eyes." Tacitus clapped his hands to gain his henchman's attention. "Timor, tug him a bit."

As Timor's men spread out and positioned themselves two near Philo's feet and two near his hands, I noticed for the first time that each rope disappeared off the table surface. I followed the line from Philo's right foot, tilted my head and spied bolted underneath at table's edge a wooden hand crank with axle, and to the axle was wound the open end of rope.

Moving to a centered place near Philo's head, Timor barked, "Give it to him," and four men turned four cranks to pull Philo's limbs in four directions. Ropes creaked. Joints crackled. Philo groaned, stretched on the torture rack.

"Now, you know the question," Timor growled while leaning with hands on table, his head above and inverted to Philo's, dripping his rank sweat onto Philo's grimacing face. "Where is Ovid? Talk now, gladiator."

"Ex-gladiator," Tacitus sarcastically corrected. Philo fought hard against his ropes. His chest expanded, belly tightened, muscles of arms and legs bulged with exertion to keep his body together. His gallantry impressed me. His defiance displeased Galeo. "Give him some leather."

From the far table Timor lifted a strap two inches wide and immediately brought it down onto Philo's chest. He struck from between Philo's arms, cris-crossing his first blow of right to left with his second left to right. A red X formed on Philo's straining pectorals as Timor skillfully delivered another pair of blows. "Talk, damn you. Where is Ovid? Where is he hiding?"

Timor received nothing but deep-throated grunts for his efforts, but Galeo urged him to try another area. "Prepare his belly."

Moving to the table side opposite Tacitus and me, Timor brought the leather down perpendicular to Philo's tightened abdomen, painting him with lines of red from just below his sternum to just above his pelvis. He skillfully whipped Philo's hard belly while avoiding his vitals, and between each blow he asked the question in one form or another only to hear low-pitched growls through gritting teeth as the response.

After about ten strikes of leather, Tacitus decided to give his men and Philo a rest so he could work on me. "That's enough," and the whipping stopped, cranks let go. "Let him think on it for awhile."

Philo lay in recovery, fingers and toes twitching, chest and belly heaving. He rapidly filled his lungs to replenish his hard-working muscles with oxygen, and while I would have preferred to sit quietly and admire him, Galeo would not allow me to do so.

"He is a strong one, Artimos, no doubt."

"This building fascinates me, Tacitus," I went off-subject as though uninterested in his interrogation drama. "How long has it stood here?"

"It dates to first century in the days of Tiberius." Galeo could not help but beam just a bit. Any feeding of the ego causes men of his ilk to temporarily forget their purpose.

"And how long has it been yours? Or is it yours?"

"A partnership arrangement. The man in question had other plans for it, but he eventually saw my road as the better to take."

"And did he find this road here in the basement, as we are?"

"Enough of your trickery." He flopped from his stool and waddled close to Philo's head, spouting threats of what was to come. "This one here will talk soon enough." He clutched Philo's ears between both of his hands, shaking Philo left to right while sneering at me. "That little show was just for tenderizing meat. Just a preparation for act two." When the voice of Tacitus issued threats, the warts of Tacitus turned fire red.

Moving to the far side of the table, Galeo grabbed hold a board that was vertical and extended to the floor. Timor and his men, apparently well-versed in the procedure, moved to the far square table. As for this board, when I saw it from my under table view after stumbling down the stairs I assumed it merely to be a support leg. There were a few holes in its center which I figured came from wood rot, but as Galeo lifted its edge straight up through a slit in the table's surface, I clearly saw that these holes were purposely drilled into the wood. Its eight inch width rose in Galeo's grasp until its four feet of length was exposed, and at that edge a metal skirt covered the wood. Bolted to this metal skirt was a swinging hinge, and as this hinge elevated two inches above the table surface, Galeo's free hand pulled a lever underneath, locking the bracketed hinge in place. Then, he let one of his assistants hold the board while he and Timor made their preparations.

"Bring me my tool and two of those," he ordered. Timor brought him a wooden mallet and two wooden clubs, handing mallet to Tacitus while keeping the clubs. "Pegs into holes. That's all this is, doctor."

Galeo inserted one of his clubs and hammered it home. About eight inches in length, its three inch diameter at one end tapered to a one-inch rounded point at the other, and after Galeo finished hammering another one he took the board from his henchman and slowly swung it towards Philo, allowing it to gently rest upon him.

Three inches of each wooden club extended above the board, four inches poked out below. The rounded points conveniently made contact with

Philo's belly, one on either side of his navel. He raised his head, peered over his chest, and then lowered again, his eyes closed in preparing himself. As for me, I locked my fingers and tried to appear calm, but I was not liking the direction we were headed. Galeo's men returned to their crank stations. Philo was again tortured with a four-way stretch while Tacitus arrogantly strolled towards me, his cruel lip curled upwards with superiority.

"You will enjoy this, Artimos. It pulverizes his insides without leaving a mark outside." Tacitus did the honors himself, turning his back to me while pressing down the board with both hands. A breathy, high-pitched grunt followed by long, deep-toned growl was Philo's reponse, as two impaling spikes buried themselves deep into his belly. Leaning towards the board, Galeo threw his abundant weight into downward pressure, while his men mercilessly stretched Philo in four directions. And again, leather to the chest was added to Philo's misery, courtesy of Timor with X patterns launched from above Philo's anguished face down onto his chest.

Just imagine it! One strong man, bound and helpless, stripped of all defenses, stretched in four directions, chest whipped with leather strap, belly impaled by wooden spikes, and Philo took it, absorbed it, dealt with it like a hero, just as he'd done on his night of initiation to the Ludus Magnus. He uttered not one word -- no pleadings for them to stop, no acknowledgement as to whether he did or did not know the answers to their questions, no falsetto screams of agony, just masculine grunts and groans of exertion and defiance. Not only did Philo take their punishment, he gave some back. Focusing all defense to his stricken abdominals gave him strength enough to gain advantage in his tug of war with the four rope men. They held on with all their might, but their profuse sweating ran straight down their arms and to their hands, loosening their grip and allowing Philo to draw up his arms and legs ever so slightly. His heels actually came off the table by a few inches for seconds at a time before the two men at the foot cranks could regain control. Best of all? Tacitus Galeo, whose physical condition was far from ideal, huffed and puffed in pressing down the belly board, his face and head hair soaking wet, his flabby arms slick and slimy.

Maybe his heart will give out, I hoped. Wouldn't that be delightful?

No such luck. He wisely sensed he was pushing himself and ordered Timor to take his place at the board. Tossing aside his leather strap, Timor came to my side of the table and continued Philo's belly torture, while Galeo moved beyond Philo's head. His fat fingers clamped around Philo's throat, and he screamed as though a madman.

"God damn you... talk! Where is Ovid?" Still clutching the throat, he lifted and banged Philo's head to the table between his words. "That... murdering... bastard...killed... my... wife... fucked... my..."

"Tacitus!" I shouted. "Stop! You're going to have a stroke." I said it to save Philo, not Tacitus.

It worked. He let go, collapsing on the table between Philo's head and right arm, his own head resting on his own arms. Galeo gasped for air, wheezing and sweating before his legs gave out and he fell to the floor. Letting go the belly board and stretching cranks, Timor and his men ran to their stricken employer while I sat watching, waiting and hoping. As for Philo, he again recovered with deep and quick breaths of air. Our eyes met. One of his winked.

Tacitus Galeo, unfortunately, also recovered enough to grunt between breaths, "I'm all right." He waved off his men. "Just let me... get on my stool... sit for awhile." He managed to get there without their assistance, doing his best to make it appear as though he never lost control. "Let's all take a rest," he commanded between still-labored breathing.

With Timor and his men filling cups full of water from the bucket between us, I sensed Galeo might be vulnerable to some teasing. "Are you getting your money's worth, Tacitus?"

"He's... (huff, puff)... a handful... (wheeze)... No question."

"Did it ever occur to you that he knows nothing about this?"

"Oh... he knows plenty... He will talk... or die silent."

"Now, I know you don't want to kill him. Look at him. Pure athlete. Pure strength. Surely you can appreciate a man like that."

"It would be a pity."

"Especially here, like this. Why don't you let me talk with him? Maybe that will help speed things along."

"Go ahead. No harm."

I ran to him as though a grief-stricken woman. "Oh, Philo!" Climbing onto the table, I knelt beside his chest, smothering it with kisses. "Please, Philo, tell them everything." My lips laid a trail of smooches between words, moving steadily nearer to his neck and face. "I can't bear to watch you suffer. Not like this. No more, Philo... Please!" I kissed his right cheek. "No man can take this." My lips pecked his right ear lobe, and I whispered secretly to him between audible to everybody *mmm* kissing sounds. "Hold on, *mmm*, Philo...*mmm, mmm*, elixir." Then came more kisses to his cheek as I moved back onto his chest with moanful pleading. "No man can take such punishment. Please, Philo! Don't make them torture you any more... I cannot bear it."

And for the first time since our arrival to this foul fortress, Philo spoke. "None of their tortures will break me. Do you hear? I'll never talk. NEVER!"

Catching the sly wink of Philo's eye, I left the table with moisture in mine. Whether my tears were real or for purpose of deceiving Galeo I cannot recall, but wouldn't tell you even if I did remember.

"I'm sorry, Tacitus. It is hopeless," said I with head sadly turning.

"Well then, Timor, you and your men should get back to work."

Philo's stretching began anew.

My, my, how I wish you could have seen Philo prepare for his belly torture. He strained his arms with renewed confidence. He expanded and thrust his chest high into the air, sucked in and tightened his belly to stone wall hardness, jutted forward his lower jaw and stared directly at me. Those beautiful cobalt eyes. Those powerful, hard-at-work muscles enhanced with his just-right covering of masculine dark hair. Those toe-curling, perfectly-sized feet with strong arches and more hair atop each toe. Those meaty fists sufficiently compacted with strength to knock out an entire row of teeth. And best of all, those ever-so-slightly turned up lips that only I could recognize as conveying confidence. All of it was focused on me! My hero. My glorious athlete. My gallant warrior. My tortured gladiator.

What does it take to describe the perfect man? What words will properly convey emotions when the gods give to you your perfect man? The man formulated in your brain as the ideal, not just in body but also in spirit? A beauty of soul that supercedes the beauty of physique? I cannot. He is my Philo. I will never abandon him. He will have to chase me away.

This time, Timor gave it everything he had, pressing down the belly board with incredible force. And for good measure, he grabbed hold the mallet and pounded the pegs deeper into muscle. Philo's sounds were pitiful, yet mesmerizing, oozing with masculine strength. Timor even went so far as to drop his mallet and drop himself below the table, kneeling on the floor while pulling down on the board with his full weight, but in reality he did this not for leverage. He did it because everything was turning white for him, and even though he didn't know what was happening or why, Galeo soon did. One by one, each of his crank turners collapsed where they stood, letting go their cranks and crumbling to the floor in an unconscious heap.

"What the hell is going on here?" Tacitus howled in bolting from his stool.

"I'm... dizzy," said Timor, who with his last moments of consciousness retaliated against the perpetrator -- me. He stood, turned and lunged towards me, clasping both of his bear paws around my throat, and had I not managed to get one set of my fingers between myself and him before he clamped on his death grip, I do believe he would have crushed my windpipe right then and there.

The good news? Philo's torture stopped and Timor's grip on me was weakening. The bad? Of the six enemies in the room, Tacitus, the man amongst them who by far was in the poorest of health, was also the only man amongst them who had not partaken of my elixir-spiked water. And what did this son of a whore do while Philo laid helpless and I struggled with a fading Timor? He picked up his mallet and proceeded to hammer away on Philo's ankle -- the left one, the one upon which we had worked so hard to restore.

With the strength of a madman I broke free from Timor, as Galeo pounded on Philo once, twice, three times and was raising his arm for a fourth when I finally reached him. I bull-rushed him and drove him into the stone wall. My hands grasped his throat. My hands slammed the back of his head into solid rock again and again until through my fog of rage the voice of Philo filtered into my brain.

"Stop! Artimos! Enough!"

I let go. The eyes of Tacitus rolled upwards as he slid straight down, his well-cushioned buttocks smacking the floor. Unconcerned with him, I lifted that hideous board off of Philo's belly, took a henchman dagger from the far table and cut Philo's ropes one by one below their knots. Next, I climbed onto the table with him, cradling the back of his head with my hand to help him sit up.

"Did you kill him, Artimos?"

"I don't know, Philo, and I don't care."

"How long before they wake up?"

"Half an hour, maybe. How bad is your ankle?"

"Hard to say. I hurt all over."

"Where are your clothes?"

"Upstairs... somewhere."

"No time to look. Here, take this dagger and cut the rope knots." As he slipped dagger between rope and wrists and ankles, I found near the wall a set of piled clothes that Galeo's henchmen had stripped from themselves. Grabbing them, I returned to help Philo sit with legs dangling off the table. "Here, this will do." I slipped it over his head and he did the rest.

"Artimos?"

"What."

"I can't walk."

"Don't worry. We're getting out of here one way or another." I turned with my back between his legs, hooked behind his knees the inside crook of my bent elbows. "Now, hold on and don't let go." With his arms wrapping my neck, I lifted him from the table, bounced him to reposition his knees for my best leverage, and we made our way for the stairs.

"I don't see any blood," Philo observed as we passed by Galeo.

"That's promising," I huffed.

Compared to Philo, physically I'm nothing, but to get Philo safely out of there, I was Hercules. Once we made it past the low clearing of the stairwell, I had us out the front door within seconds, and I turned right two times knowing that there was alley space between our building and the warehouse beside it. As I'd hoped, the carpentum was still there with horse hitched.

"Philo?"

"Yes, Artimos."

"That carpentum belongs to Livilla Galeo. It will be recognized. We being in stolen wagon of murdered woman might make it look as though we..."

"Unhitch it. I'll ride the horse with you."

Rather than trying to set Philo onto the ground and expecting him to stand one-footed while I unhitched, I decided to put him on the horse first before separating beast from carpentum. With a bend of my knees Philo's right foot touched down. Next, I turned, and taking him in my arms boosted him onto the horse's back. Belly down, he swung his good leg...

Artimos!

Yes, Philo.

Do you really think they need to know how we got on the god damned horse?

Point taken.

A Boner Book

Home Away From Home

Best we forget about the Artimos horse idea altogether, because as soon as I sat atop the thing I knew I'd never be able to ride it very far.

"Artimos, where are we going?"

"Back to the city. Where else?"

"I'll never get to the city gates. You might as well lop this thing off right here and now."

"No." He motioned for me to slide off the horse. Artimos caught me, cradled me, carried me to the back of the carptentum and sat me inside. "Wait here."

That was a good one. Like I could go anywhere. What the hell was wrong with me? Why was I being such a softie after surviving torture like a hard-ass? I guess because when you're bound in rope you do what you have to do and hope you live to tell about it. Now, we had options, and after what I'd been through, Artimos was proud to treat me like I was a helpless baby. He went back inside to fetch Tacitus Galeo, dagger taken in case he'd awakened. As I mentioned before, Artimos has plenty of strength when he finds purpose to use it, and somehow he got that limp, 300-pound slab of meat up the stairs, out the door and into the carpentum. From the looks of Galeo's heels and calves, I'd say Artimos dragged him all the way, and smartly, he'd brought with him another dagger. It was for me. He kept his.

Before shutting the door, he told me, "Keep him quiet. When we get to the gates I'll tell them I'm transporting Tacitus Galeo. I suspect Keepers of the Gate will be glad to see us, but I don't know that for sure. If things don't look good, I will tell them we've been in Ostia for a business meeting with him. Do you think you can convince Galeo to repeat that to the guards if they ask him?"

"Are you joking? He will say it or he will die silent. Isn't that what he said about me?"

We made it to the road from Ostia to Rome uninterrupted, and since it appeared Timor and his men had used nothing but the carpentum for their two trips of abduction into the city, those cavemen were left without transportation other than their own two feet. 18 miles makes for weary feet traveling at a much slower pace than ours.

"Don't move or I'll open your throat," I warned Tacitus when he began to stir. He laid on the floor. I sat on cushioned bench above him, my good foot on his chest and blade of my right-hand-held dagger inches from his jugular, ready to strike.

Galeo didn't move much, except for his facial contortions when the pain of his throbbing skull was realized. "Wh... where am I?" I kept silent, waiting for his brain to recognize and remember me. "You! Where are you taking me?"

"I'm not telling you a damned thing. Not under torture. Not now."

"Let me go, damn you. You can't do this to me."

"Really? You did this to me... and to Artimos. Why can't we do the same to you?"

"Because, I am Tacitus Gal..."

"You are shit, and that is all you are."

"Wait until my Praetor hears of this. I'll contact Aurelian! He knows..."

"Shit is for the sewer, Tacitus, and if I hear one more word out of you that is where you will go. Make one move, I cut your throat. Your important friends can fish you out, if you truly have any friends. Straight to the sewer. That is where they'll find shit like you."

Apparently, Galeo decided his life was more valuable to him than his desire to spew his loads of crap, so he shut up and laid still. Pity, because the old me was tempted to slice him and dice him just to hear the pig squeal.

"That's better. Now, when we get to the city gates and you confirm your business with the guards for entry, you will tell them if they ask that we're merchants returning with you from Ostia. Otherwise, I will gladly show them what you did to my ankle. Show them my red striped chest and belly and rope burns, and name you for what you are."

"They'll never believe you. I am a well-respected..."

"You are a whore bitch. Nothing more. This is my last warning. One more word and you're a dead tub of guts. I'll take my chances with the magistrate."

The pointed tip of my dagger pressing the fat of his second chin seemed to convince him. Galeo shut his trap.

As it turned out, no false speech from Tacitus Galeo was necessary. A decree of detention had been issued by the Praetor Urbanus in Galeo's district for both him and for Ovid. Once the back door was opened and he announced his name, two guards informed him that he would be escorted to the home of a certain magistrate to answer some questions. And, rather than wait for him to wallow his flabby self out of the carpentum, they came in and got him. Tacitus was stunned, tempted to complain, but either he was too puzzled to formulate words or too afraid of me or the guards or his future that all he could do was oink.

I myself was a bit curious as to who knew what, and so when Artimos poked his head in after Galeo and his escort had cleared the way, I probed him. "Did you tell them about our...?"

"Abduction?"

"Yes."

"No, Philo. Once they heard who was in the back they jumped right on it."

"Well, won't they now want to know what the hell we're doing in a murdered woman's wagon?"

"Not to worry," Artimos grinned triumphantly, turned his head to the right and nodded towards me. "Take a look. Guess who I've got in here."

The guard joining Artimos seemed familiar, but...

"Philo," Artimos introduced. "This is Drusus Macarius. Do you remember?"

"Hello again, Philokrates the gladiator." He removed battle helmet and stepped into the cart. "Maybe you remember this." With a growl, Drusus formed a fist and threw it into the side wall.

"You! Drusus!" I burst into laughter. "You belly punching bastard from hell. Give me that strong arm of yours." He extended his and I gave him mine.

Seemed so long ago, my first night at the Ludus Magnus, and here was the very man who gave me that beating. Back then I would have killed him if given the chance, but now I understood better how things work in Rome. A man does his duty. No questions. No remorse. And at that moment I was hoping he would make it his duty to help us get where we needed to go.

"Artimos tells me you hurt your ankle again. Did a little dance on the stairs, did you?"

"Yes. Broke my damned walking stick, too."

"Philo, seriously, did Galeo do that to you?"

"Ask Artimos."

"No need. I know damned good and well who did it. I see the burns on your wrists. Anyways, since late afternoon we've been looking for both of you. Call went out to all city battalions that Tacitus Galeo had sent men to abscond with Philo the gladiator. Nobody bothered to think you might be outside the city, though."

"Drusus," Artimos interrupted. "Who issued this order?"

"Hell, I don't know. Had to be one of the magistrates. Praetor Aulus issued the one for Ovid and Galeo."

"So you know about Ovid?"

"Officially no, but rumor is he killed Galeo's wife."

"Ok, then. He says he didn't, but Philo's the only person who's seen him after the event."

"So, Galeo sent his goons, huh?"

"Yes. Twice. Once for Philo and again for me."

"Hey, you two!" I was feeling neglected. "My ankle's not getting any smaller here."

They both looked at my swollen, bruising, bleeding and broken mess. "Damn, Philo. That is ugly. Ok, Artimos, you ride back here with him. This wagon's under detention, too, but we'll drop you off at your house. It's more or less on the way."

"Better go to the Ludus," Artimos explained. "Our house is in shambles."

"Why? Did Galeo do that as well?"

"His men did," Artimos said. "Probably looking for proof Ovid had been there, but used it as an excuse to plunder."

"My god but you and Philo have had a day of it. Ok, we're off to the Ludus Magnus. Get him fixed up."

With Drusus on horseback leading the way, one guard as coachman and another as horseman behind us with extra horse in tow, we finally entered the city. Neither of us knew the time. It was dark and the streets taken by Drusus mostly deserted. From here on out Artimos was in charge. We went directly to the Ludus Magnus so my doctor could tend to my ankle after Drusus carried my carcass inside all the way to Artimos's exam room.

"Best of luck to both of you."

"Good to see you again, Drusus," said Artimos. "Now that I know where you're stationed, I'll come pester you from time to time."

Drusus left; Artimos went to work. Lucky for you I'm telling this part, because Artimos would go into great detail about which bones were cracked and which this that or the other. Here it is: you know that knob that sticks out on the inside of your ankle? That's what Galeo crushed. His mallet struck me on that same bump however many times he hit me.

So, with my diagnosis complete, we did things in order of importance to us. First, Artimos wrapped my ankle with cold linen to stop the swelling. Next, we ate. Artimos bathed in the Ludus baths while servants sponged me. Finally, Artimos told me exactly what he needed to do for repair this time. Fortunately, the damage was opposite the side hacked by Ovid's sword.

News and rumors of Ovid, plus the truth of what had happened to me and Artimos quickly spread from cell to cell. The gladiators became agitated, and Artimos suggested to the guards that two at a time be brought into his exam room under secured escort for brief visits. Better for them to see me and hear from me than to have them start a riot with rumors.

Frankly, I didn't know I was so popular, but these gladiators treated me as though I was some sort of hero to them. Artimos said later that a freed gladiator was inspiration, an example of possibilities, their hope of a way out of slavery. Whatever, the end result for me was that rather than allowing Artimos to put me to sleep, I used the strength of those men to endure all pain. They talked to me. Gave me firm grips of resistance for when Artimos made his incisions and finagled my bones.

Using one of his special tools, he reshaped my cracked bone to the curve it was supposed to be, sewed me up and outfitted my ankle with a linen wrap followed by some sort of wet and pasty stuff. When it dried, I had a hard outer shell to protect me. Artimos estimated at least three days before I should even try to put any weight on it, as this would be the time necessary for bone to begin growing back together and hold itself in the shape he'd made.

All that could be done had been done, and with our home in shambles, Artimos and I slept right there in his medical room on surgical beds. Or at least we tried. Despite obvious exhaustion, thoughts were racing in our heads, thinking again through all the things that had happened to us. It was just a matter of who was going to ask what questions first. I did.

"Artimos?"

"Yes, Philo."

"How did you get your elixir down to that basement without any of them finding it?"

"Well, I hid it in the only place they'd never look."

"Where? Your ass?"

"Yes."

"What? I was only joking! Are you serious?"

"Of course I am. I put it in a long thin vial right here in this room before going home. Kept it clinched halfway in and halfway out."

"That strong asshole of yours."

"Ha, I suppose I'm strong enough there. All I had to do was convince Tacitus that I needed to shit. That little basement room in the dark was perfect to pull it out, wipe it off and slip it into my pocket."

"Then you put it in their water?"

"Yes. They all five were working on you, and when Galeo joined in by choking you and banging your head on the table, I opened and dropped its contents in the bucket right next to me. Damned Tacitus never drank any water, though. Another minute and Timor would've been out and Galeo never would have got to your ankle."

"No way you could have seen that coming. Me neither. The bastard."

"A man can't get much lower than that, doing what he did to you."

"What do you think the magistrate wants with him?"

"I have no clue. All I know is we'd best not report to anybody unless we have to. Never know which magistrates are honest and which are easily bought. Let them come to us, as I'm sure they will. I'm also sure Drusus will spread word quickly about your ankle and torture and who did it. Guards will be on our side in this. Make no mistake."

"How do you suppose they knew that we'd been abducted?"

"Who?"

"Whoever ordered the battalions to look for us."

"Our magistrate, I expect. Had to have come from my administrator, because nobody else knew you'd been taken."

"You told him?"

"Of course. I had to have good people working for us and hope Galeo would come back for me. After all, how else could I have found you? Galeo did it for me."

"So, if your vial scheme hadn't worked, our last hope was for the Guard to rescue us."

"Yes. I'm glad you didn't have to wait that long. Like Drusus said, those are city battalions. They stay inside the walls and man the gates. Nobody thought to look in Ostia. But what a stroke of luck to see Drusus at the Ostiensis Gate. I had no idea..."

"I know, Artimos. That's why I leave such things to your judgment. You think of everything."

"If only that were true all the time. You're the one who gave me the idea to bring Galeo with us. Another stroke of luck. That's how I should have played it to begin with."

"And to think you nearly killed him."

"Was it that bad? Ha, I guess that would have added a whole new wrinkle. Anyway, I should have known you couldn't ride a horse. I'm the doctor, but I guess I wasn't thinking like one. That ankle'd taken enough pounding for one day."

"You just wanted to get us the hell out of there before they woke up. You were thinking like you should have been."

"End result is that we made it here... safe for now. Philo, if the magistrate comes here asking us questions, we must tell the truth. We've done nothing wrong, and besides, I'm no good at doing it any other way. One lie leads to another until I can no longer remember where I started."

"I am the same way, Artimos. Not clever enough to make up stories worth a listen."

"Good."

His silence indicated his satisfaction that we were together on this and that I understood enough of what was happening to do the right thing. Now, I waited for him to either start snoring or open a new topic.

"Philo?"

"Yes."

"We should try to find Ovid. If he told you the truth he should say it to the magistrate. And remember, he was pardoned by the Emperor. He will be protected somewhat."

"I agree, but I don't know where he is."

At this Artimos quietly laughed. "That is rich. Galeo tortured you for nothing."

"Tortured us."

"Ok, not that it matters whether you knew anything or not. He will suffer for what he did. If we don't get him, the gods will."

"Hope so. As for Ovid, thinking of him sours my stomach. I want him, Artimos. I hope you understand. I'm scared for him. I don't know how or why, but I feel I must protect him. He should be with here with us."

"Don't worry, Philo. We'll find him. Do what we can to get him through this."

These words settled our minds enough to allow sleep, which I did soundly and for heaven knows how long. I was not pleased, however, when I awakened to find Artimos missing. Argo, my ex-lanista told me that Artimos asked him to look after me when he could, to make sure I didn't try to use my leg. He obviously told servants and guards, too, because they hovered constantly. The administrator said Artimos left a message on his desk saying he needed to be gone for the day, and this troubled me, but since my day was filled with curiosity and not much more, I will let Artimos tell you exactly what he did. All I did was sit and fret, wavering between being angry with him for leaving without telling me, and worrying about him, wondering if he was all right. Of what interest could that be to anybody besides me? Damn him.

A Boner Book

The Round Trip

My original plan for the day, other than taking care of Philo, was to make contact with my good friend Antonia Siculus. She having blood ties to one of the oldest patrician families in Rome made her an invaluable source for information regarding the goings-on of the rich and powerful, but an interruption came before my day even began, one that would force me to put my visit with her on hold.

A servant nudged my shoulder to awaken me, informed me that a foot messenger waited for me outside. The messenger refused to come inside for fear of being overheard, and so, grouchily, I slipped out of bed, leaving Philo to snore peacefully. With loyalty to his source worthy of praise, this courier begged to see a form of indentification proving that I was who I claimed to be before he could proceed. I did, and received my message verbally. It was from Drusus Macarius. I was to come to his garrison barracks as soon as possible. That would be right now, I thought, and so I told foot messenger my reply: Expect me by mid-morning.

It was imperative I get to our house before sunrise. I needed change of clothing; I needed money; most of all, I needed to travel there before the streets filled with people, as this would make it easier to know if anyone watched my movements. They didn't. By the time I was ready for my long walk to the city gates on the Via Ostiensis, the sun was up and another work day beginning. I easily blended into the throngs.

This garrison was built inside and abutted to the Servian Wall several feet from the gates, and my foot journey from northeast to southwest, with a few zig-zags for extra precaution took nearly two hours. Strangely, upon my arrival and request to see Drusus, the barracks guard told me rather abruptly that Macarius was sleeping, but reversed his attitude after I realized that I'd foolishly failed to announce myself first.

"I am Artimos Traius, physician at the Ludus Magnus, and Drusus Macarius wishes me to inform him personally of the condition of his good friend, Philokrates the freedman gladiator."

A plausible enough reason, I thought. It is good to be recognized and respected by those who serve the citizenry of Rome: Tribunes, City Guard, Keepers of the Gates. Drusus appeared within two minutes dressed in casual tunic and we meandered to one side of the garrison in an alley way for privacy.

"Thank you for coming so quickly, Artimos."

"Philo is sleeping. I had no other pressing issues."

"How is he?"

"He will be good, I think. I repaired the bone and outfitted him with cast. He will be unable to walk for three or four days, at least he won't if I have my say."

"Philo is fortunate to have such skilled hands taking care of him."

"And I am fortunate to have such a good friend as he... and you, Drusus."

"Artimos, Ovid is in Ostia."

"Free or captured?"

"Captured. He tried to board a ship for Sicily. It would leave at sunrise, but ticket agents alerted the Harbor Guard."

"Don't tell me... Siracusa."

"How in hell did you know?"

"His sister is there in service to an estate holder. He told me once this was the only family whose whereabouts he knows."

"Well, he didn't get there. Word was out. With all those scars he was easily recognized."

"Yes, many a time did I stitch him back together."

"He is being held for transport to Rome. I have asked the commander in Ostia to delay their trip in hopes you could speak with Ovid first. Perhaps tell him what you know about Galeo. Perhaps calm him down a bit."

"I don't know anything about Galeo, but I will try to calm him down."

"Word is that one of Galeo's servants confessed an interesting tid bit."

"What?"

"The assassin was to kill Galeo's wife, along with Ovid."

Drusus nearly had to prop me up after that one. "Well, now, that certainly throws a hot iron into the fire. That tricky bastard. None of this would have happened if..."

"I know, Artimos. We men favor Ovid in this dispute, but you must go quickly. The Praetor Urbanus demands he be delivered before sundown, and the wagon will not stop at these gates. Once he leaves Ostia, nobody sees him."

"Then I will go now. Direct me to the nearest stables."

"I have a mount ready for you in our stables. Come with me."

As I walked beside him, Drusus added some disheartening news."

"Artimos, a witness accuses Ovid of assaulting her last night. A prostitute, and according to the commander she is badly bruised and bloodied. He tried to strangle her."

"She probably tried to steal his coins. That seems to be a pattern with him. You know his head is not right."

"So I have heard. He never should have left the Ludus Magnus."

"We all tried, but Galeo used his weight. The important thing is that you have done your best for him, Drusus. Now his fate rests with the magistrate, or wherever they take him. It's what he should have done in the first place, but gladiators don't know these things, do they Drusus."

He clasped my arms in farewell, and then helped me mount my horse.

"Do what you can, Artimos. Keep him from further trouble."

Out the gate and into a medium trot I began my 18 mile journey back to Ostia. The Via Ostiensis follows very closely the Tiber, and to my right were lines of oxen on land pulling barges on the river going in both directions -- goods from ocean ships in Ostia Harbor heading towards Rome; goods from Rome destined for loading to ocean ships. Via Ostiensis itself was busy as well. Many times did I have to slow my pace waiting for wagons to meet and clear one another before I could pass. And guess what else I saw about midway there -- Timor and his four men, in chains and on foot, four dressed, one in loin cloth, all bracketed by Praetorians on horseback, one in front, two behind. None of the prisoners noticed me. Their heads looked down with eyes to the pavement as they solemnly shuffled towards the city. This I thought was a good sign, an indication that perhaps the empire of Tacitus Galeo crumbled at that very moment.

My hopes for such a scenario dimmed considerably upon my arrival to the garrison in Ostia, for the commander of which Drusus spoke did not allow me access to Ovid, not until I myself was in leg irons and riding in covered wagon for transport along with him.

Was Drusus betrayed? Or had Drusus betrayed me? Either way, my meeting with Ovid was of no use because his condition had deteriorated considerably. Seated and leaning against wagon sideboard with his legs flat, he stared blankly forward, only occasionally flashing wild eyes at me as I spoke seated opposite him with my legs the other direction. He looked at me as though wishing I would shut up, as though tempted to attack me, but then his eyes softened and returned to stare at nothing. Of course, he couldn't have done much to harm me with his wrists locked into brackets mounted on the wagon floor, but if looks could, then on occasion I do believe Ovid would have strangled me as he'd done to the prostitute. At least he recognized me just enough to leave me be, so I told him everything that had happened to me and Philo since yesterday. Maybe he absorbed it, maybe not, but everything I said to him needed to be said. And yes, I told the latest revelation regarding Livilla Galeo.

Drusus did not lie about the wagon entering the city with no stops, and unless someone was at a height greater than the wagon where metal bars allowed open air, nobody could see who was inside. We came to a stop. The door was opened inside small stables, personal stables, and we were led through a doorway into somebody's house.

Ovid and I stood in a parlor much nicer than accommodations provided to Philo and me by Tacitus Galeo. Still in leg irons, we waited with six Praetorians -- two behind us, one to Ovid's right, one to my left, and two facing us from either side of a large wooden desk.

"Good evening, gentlemen," said the man entering with papers in hand, his cream-colored toga trimmed in purple, his servant following closely behind looking Greek, looking to be a scribe. "My name is Vitellius Silanus," continued our host. "And I am Magistrate for the Caelimontium District."

Fair enough, I thought while answering his "good evening" and mentally noting his youthful appearance. I guessed him to be 30 years at most, meaning that unless my age estimation was off by about 20 years, his appointment came from Emperor Aurelian or one of his consuls. I also figured this should work in our favor, for a young magistrate working his way up the ladder of appointments and elected offices is more likely to make decisions based on facts and merit, based upon what is best for the Roman citizenry, as opposed to an old magistrate permanently stuck on the same rung, whose judgement might be easily influenced by whichever party could offer him the more lucrative bribe.

After an inspecting gaze towards Ovid, this magistrate took his seat behind his desk, his scribe sitting behind him, and Vitellius Silanus addressed me.

"You are Artimos Traius? Physician at the Ludus Magnus?"

"Yes, Magistrate Silanus."

"Please address me as Vitellius. This is an informal hearing." I didn't know there was such a thing. If so, why was his scribe scribing? For my answers, formal or informal made no difference. Addressing him as Vitellius I could do.

He made request to a guard, "You may remove his irons." And as the guard followed orders, Vitellius continued with me. "First, the records show you are the fourth generational member of your family to serve in this capacity, and I want to express my personal gratitude for your loyalty to Rome and the Empire all these many years."

"Thank you."

"Second, I wish to apologize for any discomfort and alarm I may have caused you today. Please know that everything was my doing, and that the guard at the Ostiensis Gate..." he glanced to his papers, "Drusus Macarius, had no knowledge of my plot against you. I am solely responsible, but I hope it is for good cause and that when we are finished you will understand why I did it."

"Thank you."

"Third, regarding the case of Livilla Galeo. Based upon my interviews with those involved, including her husband, Tacitus Galeo, I have forwarded my findings to the Praetor Urbanus for further witness. Fourth, on this afternoon I visited with your patient and good friend, Philokrates of Veneton, and asked him questions regarding this case."

"Was he in pain?"

My question, asked without forethought, brought a smile from Vitellius, for even though I genuinely wanted to know of Philo's condition, my asking served a more meaningful purpose. It revealed to Vitellius something of my character. I had one priority, and that was the welfare of the men in my care, especially, first and foremost, Philo. I did not give a rat's ass about murdered wives or adulterous bodyguards or vindictive husbands or power plays or struggles for financial or political superiority. I was a physician. I cared for injured men, and Vitellius knew damned good and well I had no need or desire to tell lies in regards to all these time-consuming distractions.

"No, Artimos, I don't think he was. Philo... he requested I call him Philo, seemed in good spirits and showed no discomfort, but he was fearful of your wrath should he try to stand."

"Well, if he was in pain he would not allow you to know it."

"I suspected as much. He asked about you, and I assured him that you would soon be in my care."

"Thank you. Had I told him where I was going he would have insisted upon going with me... slowing me down and risking his own health."

"Yes, your decision was sound. Now, Artimos, I will get to the heart of it. I wanted you in the wagon with Ovid as a calming influence, hopefully to prevent him from causing any more trouble for himself and others. Unfortunately, Drusus Macarius made contact with you before I could, and ironically, his purpose was the same as mine. In fact, you've been about one hour ahead of me all day long, until my courier undoubtedly passed you somewhere on the Via Ostiensis with my dispatch for the commander in Ostia."

"I'm not much of a horseman. Lack of trust, I suppose."

"Perhaps Drusus chose for you the weary nag of the bunch so as to cause you no grief. This man seems overly interested in the welfare of both Ovid and you. Why is this?"

"He was recently guard at the Ludus Magnus. Knows all of us. Admires Ovid as I do."

"I admire his courage in alerting you of Ovid's capture."

"He is a good man. Does what he thinks is just, regardless of risk."

"So I suspected. Anyway, I needed you two together. I know about Ovid's mental instability and of your failed attempts to protect him. I know of your loyalty to him and of your concern for him, but I will expect you to tell me everything you can remember so that you and I can decide what is best for him. Agreed?"

"Yes, of course, Vitellius."

"Tell me exactly when and how you learned of the murder of Livilla Galeo."

I did tell it all, from the time Brusilla came running to warn me until my exit from wagon inside the stable of Magistrate Vitellius Silanus. And believe you me, he got every minute detail of the tortures done to Philo at the hands of Tacitus and his goons. He listened intently as his scribe scribbled frantically, and when I was finished, Vitellius leaned back in his chair with index fingers touching to a point in front of his chin, the classic pose of genius in thought.

"Thank you, Artimos. Most helpful. Now, my question is this: Do you believe Ovid can function within the confines of the Ludus Magnus, either as trainer or participant or any other service you and your superiors think appropriate?"

"Yes, Vitellius, I do, provided he is given treatments to control his violent tendencies and chronic pain. The two are related, you know."

"And I know you are the man to provide him this comfort. Therefore, I will make this recommendation to the Praetor Urbanus." He stood and focused his eyes on Ovid. "Ovid of Thebes, Ovid the gladiator, you are charged with assault upon the woman known as Berenice in the town of Ostia, and you are accused of adultery with the married woman Livilla Galeo in the city of Rome. I hereby elevate your case to a hearing of questions before Praetor Urbanus, Lucinius Aulus, and order you confined to the Ludus Magnus until which time you are summoned by guard to appear before Praetor Aulus."

He stated the date for the records, and then turned to me. "Artimos, do you wish to file a grievance against Tacitus Galeo?"

"No. My statement is given. I will let the Praetor decide what best to do with it."

"Then you are free to go. My guard will escort you, if you wish."

"Yes, please. And Vitellius, did Philo file a grievance?"

"No. He said not at this time, and I told him I would allow 24 hours if he wished to do so at a later time after he spoke with you."

"Thank you."

I got my escort of one guard for our walk of five blocks. Ovid did not come with us and I never asked the reason, assuming that since he was charged with a crime they would bring him by wagon and in leg irons. Frankly, all I could think about was my reunion with Philo, and because you and I both know my version of the event will make him uncomfortable, I am finished talking for now.

Sporting Wet

Me? Uncomfortable? Hell, I couldn't wait to get Artimos sitting on my one-person bed in his Ludus Magnus surgical room so that I could molest him. Unfortunately, we didn't have anywhere else to go for the privacy needed to celebrate properly, and even here my attempts for some sort of intimacy beyond welcome-back hugs made Artimos uneasy.

He was right, of course. At any time guards or servants could and would enter this room for any number of reasons, but I was determined as always to get what I wanted.

After he had his dinner I told him, "Artimos, give me a bath."

"Haven't the servants bathed you today?"

"Yes, but that was with sponges. Take me to the baths. I want to soak." I had to tell him because he'd have to carry me. Otherwise, I would have picked him up and carried him. He finagled me so that my ankle was at water's edge while the rest of me was in. With me sitting on a shallow-water bench and Artimos crouched next to me, waterline at his neck, I got him. A hand job was good enough, and that old-time Nubian fighter at the far end either didn't know or didn't care what we were up to. Artimos got me, too. How disgustingly beautiful to watch our white balls of sperm floating around us while Artimos told me of his busy day.

"Anyway," he began his finish. "Ovid should be here any time now."

"Artimos?"

"Yes, Philo."

"I want to go home."

"Our home is a wreck. The servants are gone. And you cannot walk. What does it matter if you're in bed here or at home?"

"Tonight, you will teach me to use the crutches. I can practice here, and then tomorrow morning I go home. I will fix our house while you work."

"What about Ovid? Don't you want to see him?"

"I will see Ovid when I get around to it. Just like he did to me."

And that right there, my friends, is the dagger through the heart of our entire story. That one day alone, sitting on my bed at the Ludus Magnus wondering and fretting as to where Artimos might be, not knowing if he was safe or threatened, alive or dead, was a torture far worse than anything Galeo could hand out. I needed this man, this doctor, this cherished companion. And I don't mean the need of him caring for some pitiful cripple, which I would always be and which he would always do until one of us was dead. No, all day long I prayed he would come back to me so that I could grab him, hug him, squeeze him hard enough to send his insides squishing out his nostrils, and then I could eat his innards. That's how bad I needed him.

Is there any doubt that he granted my wish to go home? With all possible effort I won my battle over the crutches, and in our separate beds Artimos and I spent our final evening at the Ludus Magnus sleeping soundly as the exhausted men we were. Just before sunup he coerced some of the night servants to help him transport me home. On his break for lunch he brought me mine, and by the time his work day ended and he brought with him food for our dinner, most of what could be set right in our house had been, the clutter of broken and unusable now piled into one corner of each room.

"I hope you didn't overdo, Philo."

"I know better. Don't want you to punish me."

"Are you sure?"

"No."

"Well, then, let me start by removing your cast. I'm a full day early, but this is reward for all your hard work. I trust now you'll spend more time on the bed where you belong?"

"Depends on who's there with me."

"Better be me or nobody. Any idea where my tools are?"

"Whatever I found that looked medical I put on your desk."

Artimos used his little saw back and forth on me while I laid on the bed. He cut deep enough until he could crack open the cast. "What do you see?" I asked him.

"Exactly what I'd hoped." He lightly touched my new ankle knob with his finger. "Now you must be extremely careful. The bone is growing together, but still fragile."

"What is that smell?"

"Your ankle. Ready for your bath?"

"Take me quickly before I gag."

Now, I know most Romans love their public bath houses, but not me.

Having our own private tub in our house is a luxury for kings, and once Artimos had me in our tub and filled it with one bucket after another of heated water, my ankle thanked him and Artimos knew I was his captive audience.

"Philo, today word came from Vitellius Silanus, the magistrate who came to see you."

"Word?"

"Word as to why Ovid was never delivered to the Ludus Magnus."

"I'm listening."

"Vitellius sent his paperwork by courier to the home of the Praetor Urbanus, Lucinius Aulus, and then Vitellius supervised preparations for Ovid's transport and sent him along. The wagon was intercepted. Taken directly to Lucinius Aulus for a hearing right then and there."

"This Lucinius Aulus, is he a good man?"

"I know nothing about him, Philo, but usually that is good. Men who do their job properly do so with little fanfare. It's the shady ones who make known their few good deeds to distract you from the many bad."

"Makes sense. Go on."

"Apparently, while I was on the road to Ostia, Tacitus Galeo told his story to Praetor Aulus, and based upon what he heard, he ordered Galeo held under house arrest until he could hear Ovid's side of it. I think it was noble of Praetor Aulus to value Ovid's answers equally with those of Tacitus. After all, most would consider..."

"Artimos?"

"Yes, Philo."

"I know you. You're taking forever to tell me that Ovid is dead."

"Hmm. Correct, you do know me. Would you like to hear the details?"

"Please."

"Praetor Aulus sent word that Tacitus Galeo be brought to him from his house, where he was being held by Praetorian guard to make sure he stayed there. As you can guess, Ovid tried to attack Galeo when he entered the room."

"So they killed him."

"Probably had no choice. I told you what he was like."

Here Artimos paused for me, and after thinking on it awhile I realized that I was neither sad nor angry. More than anything, I think I was relieved. Seemed the best for everybody, especially for Ovid. "Well, Artimos, we fought a good fight."

"I think we lost that fight when Galeo took Ovid from us."

"But we never gave up. Did we?"

"No, Philo. We couldn't seem to get on top of it, so we spit from below."

"Damned right. Ovid fell in with a treacherous bunch, that's all."

"It pleases me you are taking this with a good attitude, Philo."

"And why shouldn't I? He made his choices. I made mine. He's dead. I have you. If not, I'd be just as dead as he is." And that is exactly how I felt about it -- damned lucky. "So, what about Galeo? What happens to him?"

"That is still a mystery. Praetor Aulus will decide when he's ready to decide, I suppose. Meanwhile, Vitellius wishes me to keep this quiet until a formal announcement is made. They're afraid the gladiators might riot if they hear about Ovid, and as you know we have games coming up in two weeks."

"Fair enough. I'm not going anywhere, so no need to worry about my loose tongue."

"And what of my tongue?"

"Yours is very talented."

"Do you think?"

"I know. Are you going to do me?"

"Can't wait. Where do you want it?"

"I'll take my punishment on the mattress, thank you."

Artimos didn't use his mouth so much. Reason is that once he got me out of the tub, dried me, bedded me and laid on top of me, I clamped onto him with both arms for that squeeze I mentioned earlier. Yes, Artimos may have been in the dominant position with me underneath; Artimos may have had advantage over me because I had to protect my ankle and couldn't move much; but Artimos succumbed to my rib-crushing bear hug. Artimos melted like butter in my fingers when I peppered his face with kisses. The shackles were off. No more burden of Ovid between us. No more me wondering what Artimos truly thought of my concern for Ovid, wondering if he ever worried that Ovid could some day replace him. Not a chance. Never had been, but now, all doubts were removed for both of us.

Once I had my fill of sliming his face with my spit, I surrendered to him. "It is good to be home..." I let go his rib cage and reached my hands towards the mattress corners, "where my doctor can experiment... do with me as he wants."

What he wanted to do was worship me as though we were back in Ostia. Me, on the table of torture, stretched in four directions, but the pleadings of Artimos in our bedroom were not the same as those used for his trickery in Ostia. Here, rather than begging for me to talk, he demanded that I defy them and their tortures. He told me to fight them, to hold my tongue, to show them what a real man looks like, what a real man can do. And with my excited penis filled to capacity with blood, expanded to the point of seeming that my skin on my cock head might split wide open from the incredible pressure inside it, Artimos sat down on my cock head and took every inch of me up into his gut. He squeezed the blood right out of me, reduced my once-powerful tool down to the size of a harmless pinkie finger. And then he relaxed his inside muscles and allowed me to refill with blood so that he could do it to me all over again.

With his fists he used my belly -- my poor, recently-impaled belly. He used it as his leverage to bounce on my penis. He planted those fists exactly where the stakes of Galeo tried to run me through, and Artimos tortured me in the most magical way possible, pressing his fists into my belly to glide his ass up my shaft until reaching my cock head, where he squeezed with all his might while slowly, powerfully, pleasurably and painfully sliding back down to sit on my pelvis.

I did what he told me. I fought my tormentors. I battled my stretch rack, flexing and expanding my chest so he could see that I was trying. His fists felt my abdomen tightening its defenses. He saw my lower jaw thrust forward, my eyes glaring at him, daring him to inflict more punishment, and when I flooded his rectum with my semen, Artimos knew damned good and well that I would never be broken. I would never be defeated. I would never disappoint him, and if he ever thought that anyone or anything could ever again interfere with the bonds keeping us together, I obliterated those thoughts by raising up, casting him off my dick and onto his back so that I could suck him off. That's right. I did it. I'm proud of it. My ankle hurt like hell but it never slowed me down. I told you I wanted to squeeze out his innards and eat them. Well, I did myself one better. I squeezed out his man seeds and ate those instead.

Uncomfortable? Tough shit. I love him. He can say and do whatever he pleases. Never again will I put him in danger -- not for anyone, and any man who threatens him or challenges him or tries to hurt him, that man will die. I don't care about their money or their power or their connections. I don't care if they nail me to the cross for doing it. I will kill any man who tries ever again to hurt my Artimos. He is mine.

You see, friends, Artimos is not the only one here who can spew the mush.

Lucky Bastard

Philo managed to get through the next several days piddling, working to restore our house. And he did so without once allowing his ankle to contact anything. I found a maidservant referred to me by one of the cleaning servants at the Ludus Magnus, and one was enough for now, days only, to market shop, to house clean and to ease my mind by having someone there with Philo during the daytime. This became especially vital when he started walking with the new stick made for him by my wood crafting friend. Within one week of his arrival home, Philo returned his crutches to me and was 80 percent back to where he had been before Tacitus Galeo's interference.

As I suspected, the character of Praetor Lucinius Aulus was just and honorable. Announcement was made that he and other dignitaries would attend service for Ovid of Thebes next day, and it would be done upon the Ludus Magnus field of practice. One dozen Tribunes, two dozen Praetorians, and nearly three dozen from ranks of the City Battalions accompanied the toga-clad magistrates, Senators, Consuls, Aediles and Praetors, as all gladiators, servants and staff of the Ludus Magnus surrounded the funeral pyre built center field. Lucinius spoke about Ovid's heroic exploits in the arena, spoke of his own deep sorrow regarding Ovid's end and his unwitting participation in its occurrence. He placed the coin into Ovid's mouth, fare for the ferryman, Charon, to take Ovid across the River Styx to begin his new life in the Underworld, and Lucinius did not give Ovid the standard obulus for his fare, but the aurus, which would buy him a better seat on the boat. This gesture properly honored a man who had so often and so courageously pleased the gods with his dramatic skills in the arena. Perhaps, too, it in some small measure softened their disappointment with us for failing to protect him.

Chosen to light the pyre, Philo did this honor and we all watched with silent reverence as Ovid's former body sprinkled its ashes onto the Ludus Magnus field. As it turned out, there was no need to fear Ovid's friends. Security, of course, is always necessary but many of the guards in attendance volunteered for the duty, including Drusus Macarius, while many more who wished to be there were turned down. Gladiators and servants remained solemn throughout the service, and whatever thoughts of anger or outrage they may have felt were internalized. After all, for a slave, speaking against the Empire and its system of justice is tantamount to a patrician exposing the identity of a spy sent within enemy ranks. It must not happen. It is treason, punishable by death.

Because the announcement of Ovid's death came two days after the event but with no mention made of Tacitus Galeo, I decided to make contact with my aforementioned lady friend, Antonia Siculus, to find out what the inner circle knew about him.

My relationship with Antonia began in the days when her future husband Gemellus and I studied chemistry together under the same tutor -- my interest being interactions with human blood, his being with water. Gemellus became Aedile in charge of the Claudia and Anio Aqueducts, the filteration of water through the cisterns, and maintenance of the water distribution system throughout the city. Antonia married him for his brain, not his bloodlines, for she had enough patrician blood to accommodate both of them. In fact, Gemellus, Antonia and her family were to sponsor the upcoming games. Through marriages and births that would take me an entire chapter to explain, Antonia came from the family of Amelia Paullus, who married Publio Cornelius Scipio Africanus, the Scipio who in 201 B.C. defeated Hannibal and others during the 2nd Punic War, finally ending Rome's rivalry with the Carthaginians and taking for the first time Rome's reach of empire south of the Mediterranean. This historic victory was to be remembered and celebrated in the Amphitheatrum nine days forward.

Gemellus and I became great friends before he met and courted Antonia, and her joining our friendship only enhanced it. When taken separately I adored each of them; taken together I cherished every moment with them.

Antonia's mornings usually found her at the Quintus Market situated near the Tiber, where a specialty section attracted women who didn't need to shop but did. Here were the finest linens and wools for the making of dresses and robes; rare foodstuffs, from meats, cheeses and wines to herbs, teas and spices, all expensively shipped in cold storage from all parts of the Empire; and stunning jewelries hand crafted by the finest artisans from Greece, Egypt, Persia and beyond. Antonia cared little about these niceties. She left such decisions to her maidservants. Her reason for browsing here was strictly informational, and because she knew that I cared little about such gossip under normal circumstances, Antonia had no doubt as to why I sent a messenger to her home requesting an invitation to lunch. She replied yes, next day, their house, half hour past noon, and my walk from the Ludus Magnus took 15 of the 60 minutes alloted to me.

"Artimos! You darling man! Kiss me now!" We did, my lips to her cheeks left then right. "Why have you been avoiding us? We haven't talked since the Vespasian games."

"True. I am guilty, but for good reason."

"Good reason indeed. Come with me. We'll lunch on my balcony." The day was perfect for such a setting, featuring bright sunshine of early June with cooling breeze of gone-by May. Antonia always looked good in white, her skin nearly as white to match, and all enhanced by her contrastingly black brows and head hair, its length to her shoulder blades when gathered by pin behind her neck. Handsome streaks of sunlit purple highlighted her locks while matching the purple of her always-cheerful eyes.

Knowing that I would be punctual, and knowing that my time was limited, Antonia had her servants set our table moments before my arrival with meal ready on her open air balcony, the trickling sound of fountain-recycled water directly below us in her backyard garden. This also gave her reason to avoid the low table and lounge cushion set up most Romans use so that I could sit in straight back chair. Much better for the spine, and it was good to see Antonia and Gemellus were following my advice. Everything Antonia did was perfect, and because she naturally exuded energy, joy and spirit, one could not be in her presence without feeling the same.

"Antonia, tell me of Gemellus... his health. Is he foolishly trying to hide any discomforts from us?"

"No, Artimos. I truly believe he is fit as can be. That juice you have him drink each morning seems to have cleared his colon. No more cramps, and his bowel movements... well, no need for me to ruin our meal."

"My dear lady, I am a physician. Remember? I am immune to offenses of nature. Seems I have in my pocket... yes, here it is. More burberry for his juice." I set on table the vial of concentrate I'd prepared in my work office for Gemellus before taking a second bite from my delicious sandwich of ground fish, garlic and chopped tomato. "Now, Antonia," I continued with mouth full, lack of time an excuse for my rudeness and her forgiveness, "tell me about your health since our last visit."

"There is nothing to tell. Honestly, Artimos, you have us both on the perfect diet. You are very talented at your work."

"So is your husband, our water has never tasted more fresh. It is like the spring's source is right outside our door, rather than 60 miles from here in the countryside."

"Our? Oh, yes, you absconded with that glorious gladiator, Philokrates. Took him away from the rest of us. Tell me, is he as wonderful up close as he was on the arena floor?"

"More so. The physical is a given, but his spirit is indestructible."

"And contageous. You have caught his disease, Artimos. I can feel it."

No pretensions here. This is one of many reasons why I loved Gemellus and Antonia, for whereas it was customary for the elite to regard gladiators past or present as social pariahs, even though they admired them from the safe distance of their arena seats, my friends accepted and enjoyed citizens based on merit, not standing. If they were personages of that ilk, I myself would not be allowed to her table, that trace of Greek I mentioned being the cause.

"It cannot be helped, Antonia. I hope to die from his disease."

"So, speaking of death, are you assisting with his plans for the perfect murder?"

"Murder?" I inflected my word as a question, playing the fool because she wanted me to, but I accompanied my feigned shock with a knowing smile, which she also required from me so that she could continue.

"There seems to be a long line growing in regards to a certain widower husband. Most think his poor dead wife's family has been more than generous, but considering the three people who actually saw what happened are now dead, they had little choice but to leave him be, provided of course he forfeit all of his assets to them... his house, his businesses, his property holdings, his guards, slaves and gladiators."

"That is tragic. One might think a man stripped of everything would prefer to banish himself to the hinterlands."

"Most would, I agree, but only if that man was honorable, if that man had an inkling of integrity... or a soul. Apparently, this man has none of that. He thinks so low of himself that he has taken employment with one of his former business partners, as a lackey, mind you. It is all that any decent person would dare offer him."

"I'm sure that this decent person was amazed when our widower accepted such a lowly position after having been for so long so high and mighty."

"Perhaps this decent person has plans to find our widower a lower position yet."

"Perhaps nobody would mourn such a happening."

"Perhaps perhaps no longer applies."

My Antonia, so delicious, so full of priceless gab. She placed her right hand atop my left and squeezed lightly. "Artimos, the sister of this man's wife is one of my dearest friends. I do believe you met her at one of our parties."

"I do believe I did."

"It is her wish that you and Philo receive something for your suffering, and for your gallant attempts to right this wrong."

The final portion of my sandwich was in my mouth being ground between my teeth, and after settling back in my chair, I swallowed and wiped my lips with the linen provided. "Does she await my answer on this day?"

"Yes, my dear. Certain assets are being distributed as we speak."

Damn it to hell, how I wished Philo could have been there with me. What could he want? Nothing? Everything? What did I want? What would give me a sense of justice? What could satisfy the both of us?

"Antonia, there are five men who come from, I'm guessing, north of the Danube. They served as guards and..."

"We know exactly which five. They were to be auctioned tomorrow, but we can cancel their sale."

"Do, please. Philokrates will be a superb lanista. I believe these five can make us very wealthy men."

"Excellent! I will send word to you as to when they can be delivered to the Ludus Magnus. Having them as slaves will give Philo purpose."

Purpose indeed, thought I, but before I could congratulate myself, Antonia added something else to the mix. "Artimos, the building in Ostia, do you want it?"

"That monstrosity? What ever would we do with it?"

"Think, Artimos. Think of its location. Even if you had it demolished, the lot upon which it sits is worth more than the effort."

She was right, of course. The offer was beyond generous and only a fool would turn it down. "Fancy that!" I exclaimed. "Philo and I, high-powered owners of property. I guess it's never too late to learn a second profession. We'll take it."

"Thank you, Artimos. I will have her send over the paperwork for you to sign as soon as everything is in order. Just think. You will own a piece of history. That fortress predates the harbor and island built by Claudius. It could be a museum, perhaps."

"There's an angle. A showplace to liven that town up a bit." I stood, she stood, and we hugged. "Philo and I are most grateful. Please tell your friend. And after your games for Scipio, you and Gemellus must come to visit us. By then we should have things back to normal enough for entertaining."

"We would love that, even amidst shambles. Gemellus misses you, but he knows as well as I that helping Philo has required much of your time."

"And how, but a good investment, I believe."

"The steal of a lifetime, dear Artimos. You are the luckiest man alive."

With no argument to present for that one, I proceeded to my next order of business. "Antonia, before I go, there seems to be one more item in my pocket... yes, here it is." I handed her paper upon which I had written many names.

"You angel! I was wondering if you would think of us."

"The left column lists my favorites in order, top to bottom. The right column is for those who more than likely will perish or wish they had."

She scrutinized my list of gladiators and their rankings, and then kissed my cheek. "I knew you'd come through for us. Now we can pair them off properly. With our wagers, Gemellus and I might break even!"

"It's a bit early, still nine days away, so send me your pairings when you have them ready. Friday before I will send you my modified list for injuries or any other changes."

"Will do it. Give Philo my best, even though you rudely keep him for yourself... haven't even let us meet him, you selfish devil. By the time you're finished there will be nothing left of him."

"Why, Antonia... what ever do you mean?"

I knew my visit with Antonia would be productive information-wise, but who could have imagined the bonuses that came with it? Not I. My remaining afternoon seemed to never end. I could not wait to tell Philo our good news, nor could I wait for the reward I would expect and he would give.

Natural Law

Artimos always told me the life of a freedman could take many twists and turns. Heaven knows that in my eight months of freedom I'd already had my share. He said that the life of a slave has but one thing going for it: a slave never has to make decisions. His master speaks; he reacts.

On the other hand, a freedman enters his new world as though a child. There are joys and there are dangers, neither of which he knows anything about. There are some people who spend their lives spinning webs and stepping on others in order to climb their way up, but, according to Artimos, it is a foolish game to play. Eventually one of those people stepped on will trip you and down you will fall. No, the Artimos way is to do right by your fellow citizens. Treat them as you'd expect them to do to you, and all will be good. Sure, you might get stepped on. You might get hurt, but if you persevere, if you take the high road, then somehow, somewhere, somebody, whether you know them personally or not, whether they walk your road or the low, will exact your revenge for you. They will trip whoever hurt you, because it is natural law that those who do evil will inevitably tumble with a mighty thud. It is a force just as unbreakable as the law that keeps our feet on the ground and buildings from floating through midair.

I call it the Artimos religion, and every day I give thanks to him because the damn thing works.

That being said, the fact Galeo still lived was my first true test of faith, but it was helpful to think that, as Artimos put it, taking from a man everything that is important to him, forcing him to grovel amongst those he once mocked and abused, is to him a fate worse than death. It is a walking death, and any honest man would end his own life by his own hand. Galeo alive proved to all that he was no such man.

You better believe I put those slaves into training. They already knew the skills of soldiering, sword and shield work and such, but still we had a tight schedule to keep in order to get them ready for Scipio's games. I contracted with Argo Baltius, my lanista, turned them all over to him except for one -- Timor. He stayed with us, in leg irons of course, and we put him to work repairing the gouged walls and other damage he and his men had done to our house. He seemed agreeable to this. Why shouldn't he? We treated him fairly, fed him well to keep him strong, and frequently reminded him he could just as easily be thrown into the arena to fend for himself. Even though he kept his mouth shut like we told him and did good work on his repairs, we could not by any means trust him. He was allowed no clothing so that if he did break away he'd stand out in the crowd for a quick recapture. He was chained at night with leg and wrist irons, plus a neck collar with chain attached to water pipe in the bathroom. He could break it, but we'd hear it.

The games for Scipio would come on Saturday and my men were ready on Thursday, or at least Argo said they were. He arranged transport for me so that I could watch a special demonstration on the Ludus Magnus fields, and their performance was superb. Argo had taught them well the art of showmanship and their skills matched those of men who'd trained for months.

"Argo, you deserve a bonus," I congratulated while dropping some of my arena floor coins into the palm of his hand. "With our wagers on them, you might start thinking of your retirement."

"Don't know, Philo. What would I do if not this? Might as well lay down and die."

"Don't do that. There'd be no more need to see the games without your gladiators in the fight. Make it a nice inheritance, then. You can die here doing what you do."

That evening Artimos worked on finalizing his list for Gemellus and Antonia, who I now eagerly wished to meet, but Artimos said after the games. They were too busy, he was too busy, and I was too nervous, the jitters of a first-time owner of gladiators.

An unexpected interruption came soon afterwards in the form of two men, one well-dressed in woolen tunic with leather belt, the other dressed in plain brown cloth and rope belt. With Timor upstairs at work and me still slow-moving in use of walking stick, Artimos answered their knock.

"Sirs, I beg audience with Artimos the physician and Philokrates the gladiator. My name is Frontenus Nervo, owner of Vallo Trading and Import Company."

Remember those high-priced Quintus Market items Artimos told you about? Frontenus Nervo supplied the goods. Leaving his bodyguard outside the door (I saw outline of dagger in his pocket before he left the room), Nervo accepted a seat on our new sofa while declining Artimos's offer of drink from our restocked kitchen. Two straight back cushion seat chairs faced him from the other side of our table. We sat here.

"First of all," Frontenus began, "I wish to thank you for your efforts on behalf of Ovid the gladiator. He thrilled us for many years and news of his tragic end was very sad."

"Seems everything that could go wrong for him did," answered Artimos, who I allowed as always to do most of our talking.

"True. Some chose to exploit him with no regard for his well-being. The reason for my visit is somewhat related to this incident."

"How so?"

"It is my understanding that you have come to possess the building in Ostia, the old grain exchange building where Philokrates was taken."

"And I."

"Yes, forgive me, Artimos... where you both were taken."

"It is true. An unexpected gift it was."

"Gentlemen, I would like to either purchase from you this building, or lease from you all or part of this building."

"For what purpose?"

"Tradition. It has been my family's property for three generations. Our patriarch worked there in the days of Tiberius, when it functioned as a bartering house for traders of grain. I myself housed my offices there until... well, let's say I made a bad decision in taking on an unscrupulous partner."

"Philo, it seems you and Frontenus Nervo have something in common. Which instrument of torture did he use on you, Frontenus? The cross? Stretch rack?"

"Instrument? No, my torture predates all of that. It sounds as though he has upgraded the facility. What did he do to you, Philokrates?"

"Please call me Philo. I was roped and stretched on a round table, whipped with a belt, and stakes were ground into my abdomen."

"Perhaps you two men should compare scars," Artimos suggested. "See which one of you got the worst of it."

Artimos took my hand while I stood so I could raise my clothing overhead and off. Nervo stood and did the same, as we scanned one another's loin clothed bodies. My impalement scars were faint circles of tan barely visible, while my whipping scars faded lines of pink soon to be gone.

Nervo either approached 50 years or already was there. Short and squat, his belly was slightly extended but still firm, as were his pectorals, arms and legs. The top of his head was bare, silver hair on the sides and back. His nose was broken at least once, while his chest and belly were covered with thick, partially black but mostly silver hair. No amount of hair could hide the permanent lines criscrossing his back, belly and chest, fat, hideous scars the color of uncooked meat.

"You suffered more than I, Frontenus. What did they do? And how long has it been?"

"Nearly four years now. I was roped from the rafters in the basement. Suspended by my wrists." He raised both arms to demonstrate their 12 inch separation. "I was whipped by thin leather, cut me to pieces, made me a bloody mess. And when they got bored with that they used their fists, mostly on my belly, no bones, but as you can see one got careless and cracked my nose." He lowered his arms and leaned closer to inspect me. "I am surprised your marks have healed so cleanly, Philo. Did the doctor's salves reduce your scarring?"

"No, Frontenus," Artimos answered for me. "My salves helped calm inflammation, but Philo's tormentor claimed he wished to leave no marks. The strap used for beating was wide and pegs speared into his belly made of rounded wood."

"Oh, I see. He must have perfected his methods. My scars will never leave me, even my wife finds them repulsive. Guess you could say our antagonist took from me my bedroom life along with everything else."

Artimos approached the pitiful man, clasped his hands onto Nervo's shoulders. "I am certain you fought him best you could. I only wish my elixirs could have helped you, as they did Philo. I do believe he intended to kill us both."

"Had you known me at the time and been able, I'm certain you would have done exactly that, good doctor." They separated and Nervo sat on the sofa, rubbing his temples with right hand fingers and thumb. "Holding my daughter hostage is what finally broke me. I could not bear to see her delicate skin manhandled, the blade of dagger held to her throat. Her screams, her whimpers, it was all too much."

"Frontenus, it is too late to reduce the size of your scars, but I do know of a cream that, if used daily for several weeks, will dim their color from red to pinkish-tan."

"Artimos?"

"Yes, Philo."

"Do you have some here?"

"Upstairs in a jar."

"Well, don't tell him, go get it. And chain that slave to the bed while you're up there."

While Artimos ran his errand, I told Frontenus to follow me. On the floor near a low table we rarely used (it was a struggle for me to get down there and Artimos refused to risk injuring his spine) several cushions were scattered about.

"Frontenus, line those on the floor three by three... no, long ways... make yourself a bed. Perfect. Now lay on those. We'll get you started with your treatment."

By the time Artimos returned with his jar of paste, I had Frontenus properly positioned. The cushions supported him from underneath his thighs to his head, heels on the floor, hands beyond his head also on the floor. I liked him. His torso was thick and sturdy, athletic like a wrestler, and in my eyes his scars had already disappeared. "Help me down," I told Artimos, and with me kneeling to his left and Artimos to his right, Frontenus received paintings from our index fingers. We followed each line, dipping our fingers into paste, transferring paste onto scars.

"Do this every day," instructed Artimos. "Preferably right after bath when your skin is soft."

"Perhaps your wife will do it for you, Frontenus."

His eyes were closed, and although he still wore the serious face of a businessman, he obviously very much enjoyed the attention he was getting, especially when I lingered on the scar intersecting his left tit. "Maybe she will have a new reason to take interest in me, Philo."

"It seems you are thinking of her right now," I observed. "Artimos, there is a bulge in his loin cloth. Remind him of what he will feel when his wife takes care of him again, as she soon will."

And while Artimos exposed Nervo to perform his magic on him, I tended to the wounds on his skin and the wounds in his brain, both given to him by Galeo. "I am impressed, Frontenus," I whispered. "Despite your years, your body is strong. No fat on you... all muscle. Only a hero could take what you went through. Glorious, Frontenus, that's what you are. A beautiful, virile, masculine..."

There is little doubt that Frontenus Nervo had received no adoration from anybody in the four years since his torture, because he flooded Artimos's gut before Artimos could even get into a good rhythm. And, considering that Artimos fought to avoid choking, something which he never did with me, Frontenus must have been keeping his seed for himself all that time, too.

"Now, Frontenus," I told him, "tomorrow night you give your wife this jar and spread yourself out on the floor atop cushions just like you did here. No woman can resist, certainly not one who's denied herself of you for four years. Now, get on your hands and knees so we can treat your back and then we'll resume our business talk."

I often wonder if he was expecting one of us to plug his bare behind as part of his therapy. Neither of us did, but no matter, Frontenus stoically took our treatment of healing paste to his horrific scars, never smiling, never acknowledging either favorably or no the trick we'd perpetrated on him. And this is how it should have been. What happened benefitted all of us, and besides, I knew from the moment he entered our home that he followed our religion.

His treatment completed, Frontenus stood with a "thank you both," put on his loin cloth, his tunic, his belt, and then returned to sit on our sofa with his jar of paste in hand.

"Frontenus," I joined him on the sofa still in my loin cloth, "no man can take what you endured. No man should have to. The building is yours. We have no use for it."

"Name your price."

"There is no price. We are gifting it to you."

"No you are not!" He stood as though I'd insulted him. "You earned this property. Both of you men suffered there. It is your right."

"You suffered, too. You endured far more than we did. Sit down and calm yourself." While he did as I told him, I used my Artimos training to make another offer. "How's this, Frontenus? We will add your name as partner. Three-way ownership."

"What amount do you want for buying into this partnership?"

"You already paid it, taking their whip, taking their fists. I feel we are kinsmen. You are free and clear. Either you accept the building this way or you refuse it. No more talk."

Nervo's stern, business-like expression finally cracked, the corners of his mouth turning up just a tad. He extended his arm, clutched his fingers to my shoulder. "I cannot tell you the joy you brought to me on that day."

"What day?"

"The day for Emperor Vespasian... and Claudius Gothicus... in the arena. It is the first time I have shed tears since I was tortured in my own building."

"It is your building again, Frontenus. Which part do you want?"

"The second floor is partitioned for offices. That's where I..."

"Then the second floor you will have. Resume your operations from there as they were four years ago."

"Frontenus," Artimos took over. "I will have revised papers of ownership drawn tomorrow and sent to your market office. Agreed?"

"I will sign and have them sent to the Ludus Magnus."

"Perfect. Now, since you are in the same business, do you happen to know which company hired our antagonist?"

"It is my company. I did it as a favor to Praetor Lucinius Aulus at his suggestion. My new employee was put to work offloading river barges for my market. Hard work, that. Soon his fat belly will be withered to where it began."

"If his heart does not explode first," said the doctor.

"Yes, that would be a pity." Frontenus stood for joining of arms, first with Artimos, and then with me. Our farewell progressed to a hug because Artimos was right -- we and Frontenus Nervo had much in common.

Prior to Nervo's arrival, Artimos and I'd hardly discussed what to do with our building. Both of us were so focused on the Scipio games that the subject rarely came up, but I knew sharing it with Frontenus Nervo had to be done. That's why I offered it without asking Artimos even though he was sitting right there. And do you think he questioned me after Frontenus left our home? A smile and kiss is what I got from him. Who better for us to partner with? We knew nothing about the merchant business, grain business, or any other business. Nervo's empire was built on integrity, not intimidation and trickery. More importantly, my move came naturally from my religion. The Artimos religion.

Scipio Africanus

Philo had several seating options for viewing Scipio's games. He could join our new business partner in the primest of the plebeian tiers; he could sit with Magistrate Vitellius Silanus and his seemingly-ever-more-frequent companion, Drusus Macarius; he could even join the sponsors, Gemellus and Antonia Siculus, who he finally got to meet when they stopped by the Ludus Magnus to bless all combatants before leaving for the arena. Their seats were best of the day adjacent to the Emperor's box, but Philo declined all three.

"Frontenus is surrounded by his employees, including the tub of guts whose name we don't speak. Although I've forgiven Drusus for all those belly punches, I still am tempted to punch him in the kisser for old time's sake. If I made him ugly Vitellius might abandon him. Antonia's entire family is with her. I would be nervous without you there to keep me from saying something that might offend them. So, I'm staying with you, which is what I'd do even if Emperor Aurelian himself were here and he asked me to join him."

"I think that last refusal is a lie," I joked with him. "No man turns down the Emperor who gave him his freedom, but still, I appreciate the lie."

Aurelian truly was absent, too busy with the supervision of his new city walls being constructed beyond the ancient Servian Wall. In fact, the Amphitheatrum was not even half full, 20,000 at most, for not only were the triumphs of Scipio nearly 500 years past, for some absurd reason historians tended to emphasize Hannibal and the Carthaginians when retelling the tale rather than the brilliant maneuvers of Scipio.

Imagine it! Hannibal, the eventual loser, getting all the attention just because he used elephants to scare people. Scipio turned the tables on that, ordering his buglers to blast their horns to scare the elephants. The poor frightened creatures bolted in retreat, trampling a good portion of Hannibal's soldiers in the process.

Because Gemellus, Antonia and her family were on a budget, they opted for more contests between men and no animal hunts. So many of these wild beasts had been slaughtered in the arena over centuries that many favorites were becoming harder to find and very expensive to import. Besides, Gemellus and Antonia long ago adopted a mind set similar to mine: What is the joy of seeing frightened, starving beasts thrown into a contest with little chance of victory? It's not as though they were criminals who'd perpetrated some heinous act against the Empire. We preferred to see athletic competitions, and for one-sided slaughters we wanted genuinely bad men who deserved their inevitable fates. Heaven knows there will always be an endless supply of those. And they by all means should provide us with free entertainment.

And so, after the procession began our festivities, the arena floor was transformed into the field at Zama, North Africa, complete with replica of Carthage made small to represent its distance from the field of battle. Elephants were represented by custom- made likenesses of wood frames with woolen coverings dyed grey, all on rollers and maneuvered by slaves on foot hidden inside the structure. Buglers also walked inside to blast out their hideous cries.

I thought their replicas looked damned good. Sure, real elephants might have been more dramatic, but how can you choreograph a wild beast? And besides, what of the mess? Have you ever seen the size of their feces?

Most of the injuries coming to me were broken limbs from being run over by model elephants. While I worked resetting bones and outfitting with splints, Philo stood in shadows just back from the floor's main entrance cheering for Scipio's legions, and as the two-hour battle came to an end he tucked his walking stick beneath his arm and leaned against the wall to applaud each group of warriors exiting the stage.

After the noon-time break for lunch complete with the round-robin contests of unprotected criminals fighting and killing one another until one remained, the gladiatorial pairs began their matches. Starting with a group of eight, four pairs did battle until one was defeated and replaced by a new pair. This continued until 32 gladiators had performed their best, and my work now shifted to addressing injuries of slashes, stabbings and impalements. Despite my duties, I managed to notice the beaming smile of Philo as Argo joined him to watch their newly-acquired warriors outfitted for battle by Ludus Magnus guards. The four were to be Thracians, the most heavily-armored, while two more gladiators of experience would join them on the arena floor: one Secutor, the fish, and one Retiarius, the netter.

The final pair of 32 finished their battle, a Retiarius killed by Thracian, and with six men given their weapons for the grand finale, Philo came to my blood-soaked triage center where I caught my breath, my work finished for the time being.

"Artimos, I am more nervous now than when I myself performed."

"I'm certain your men will do well. Argo is the finest lanista in all the Empire."

"Will you watch with me? Hold me up in case I collapse? In case they embarrass me?"

"If you don't mind being smeared with blood."

As the six entered the arena to make their salutes and processions, Philo and I joined Argo on the lip of the floor, in the sunshine with a perfect view of the action. But much to my surprise, the six did not break into three pairs. They broke four against two, Philo's Thracians against the Retiarius and Secutor.

"Philo, who arranged this battle?"

"Gemellus and Antonia."

"That's not how they had it drawn up on my list."

"They altered it this morning and suspended all wagering."

"Why?"

"More excitement."

"This is not right. You give your men unfair advantage," I admonished.

"It's the privilege of being a hero. Right, Argo?"

"Right."

This was the first time Philo had ever disappointed me. Honestly, I was shocked he could stoop so low, and even more surprised that Gemellus and Antonia went along with it.

The first blow came from one Thracian, as the fish and netter immediately assumed postures of defense. Sword struck shield of Secutor and Secutor struck back with his sword to Thracian shield. After absorbing the blow, however, the Thracian shield fell from his hand. Actually, it fell from its handle, because the Thracian's hand still held it firmly in his grip. As he raised his sword to strike back, its blade flew through the air landing behind him, leaving him with sword handle in one hand and shield handle in the other. Secutor thrust his sword straight through Thracian's exposed chest, a death blow.

As this was happening, three Thracians attacked Retiarius, who deftly side-stepped and darted between the heavily-armored, slow moving warriors. Another Thracian shield fell to the floor; another blade flew threw the air.

"They seem to be having equipments problems. Eh, Argo?" Philo nudged with an elbow.

"Yes. It does appear to be an issue."

With Secutor joining his Retiarius mate, three Thracians struggled to survive as their metal grieve leg protectors fell from them with each step. Two shields fell, two blades sailed through the air until all protection for Thracians lay uselessly on arena floor.

"Artimos," Philo ribbed me, "I hope you were not foolish enough to wager on my gladiators. They are not fit to be in the arena. And Argo, I want my money back. You are the worst of the worst. And you call yourself a lanista?"

"Some men cannot be trained, Philo. I did my best."

"I can see that you did. Don't you think so, Artimos?"

"You evil, evil men." We watched the three remaining of Tacitus Galeo's henchmen run uselessly from one wall to another in nothing but sandals and loin cloths, while Secutor and Retiarius slowly stalked, waiting for them to tire. "If I were not soaked in blood I would hug you both."

"Please don't," said Philo. "We wouldn't want to miss seeing their end."

As for the sparse crowd, they seemed to know exactly what was happening and why. All stood to ridicule the three, some shaking their fists in anger, others laughing with great joy, and as one surrendered himself by laying on the arena floor with index finger pointed to the sky, all demanded Retiarius finish him. A trident through the belly would do the trick, although it would be a painfully slow end.

From behind us came clanking of metal. Sixteen gladiators, those victorious in their pairs matches, emerged from the Ludus Magnus tunnel without weapons and marched right past us, returning single file to the arena floor. And by the time the sixteenth man entered, Philo's two antagonists had been herded to the center and surrounded by Philo's friends.

"Will you do the honors, Philo?" asked Argo.

"Artimos, should I limp or would you like to carry me?"

"This is your day for justice. Take your walking stick and..."

A booming voice from behind us caused Argo, Philo and me to freeze where we stood. "Make way for Emperor Lucius Domitius Aurelianus."

We turned. Argo dropped to one knee while I assisted Philo in trying to do the same.

"Stand up!" he commanded from the center of twelve Imperial Guardsmen flanking him six by six. We did stand, but at attention, as the guards angled to form a wedge. Emperor Aurelian moved directly towards Philo, who was centered with me on his right and Argo on his left.

"Philokrates of Veneton..."

"Philokrates Aurelianus," Philo assured the Emperor that he'd proudly assumed the name of his master who freed him, and I cringed at Philo's interrupting the man.

"My friend," Aurelian smiled, placing his hand to Philo's shoulder and nearly causing the cripple to lose balance, until Argo and I steadied him.

"Nine months ago I came to Rome as ruler and you honored me in the arena behind you. Now, you again have done a great service to me and our citizens." Aurelian removed his hand and took one step back. "Artimos Traius, you have served the Empire faithfully for well over twenty years, and now you also were participant in thwarting the evil plot against me and the citizens of Rome."

The look of stupidity on our faces brought a rather sinister smile from the Emperor, as he strategized his explanation. "I refer to the plot of one Tacitus Galeo, whose intentions were to circumvent the construction of my new city walls. He plotted to rob from the treasury, contracting with unscrupulous suppliers to deliver inferior stones containing shale, mortar mixed not of volcanic ash but of wooden ash, while taking from my construction fund the full amounts for his weakened product. Can you see how he thought me the fool? Can you hear the laughter as my wall crumbles faster than I can build it? Your efforts exposed him. His suppliers have talked, and now, Philokrates Aurelianus, I wish you to honor me with Roman justice... for myself... for you... and for Artimos."

A sword was brought by servant behind the Emperor's entourage. He removed it from sleeve, turned it, and presented its handle to Philo. "My battle sword. With this you must spill their blood. Go, you have many friends waiting."

Philo took the sword of Aurelian, but with his left hand took hold of his Emperor's hand. Bowing, he kissed the ring of Lucius Domitius Aurelianus, turned, and with his walking stick limped into the arena.

Twenty thousand cannot match the roar of fifty, but they tried.

Argo and I stepped forward ten paces to get a clearer view, but Emperor Aurelian did not. This was Philo's moment of glory, not his. Philo entered the circle of gladiators, demanded both men stand. One did, one stayed on his knees, pleading. For standing to receive the death blow with courage, Philo granted a quick end, severing the head with a pinpoint slice of the neck from right to left. For whimpering like a coward, Philo killed ugly, bringing Emperor's sword straight down to the top of the head. The skull split, torso fell, arms and legs twitched until life was no more.

Long ago had Tacitus Galeo tried to make his escape. Seeing mysterious equipment failures befall his former henchmen, Galeo charged from his seat only to be tripped and secured by loyal employees of Frontenus Nervo. They held Tacitus, forced him to watch Philo dispatch the final two of his four thugs, and now, as Philo received congratulatory salutes from his gladiator companions, Nervo's men unceremoniously tossed 300 pounds of terrified swine over the wall and onto the wooden floor. Tacitus Galeo landed with a thud. He twisted and broke his leg upon impact. He rose to all fours, pathetically dragging himself to no place of importance, no place of any use.

Galeo's performance could not have been better if scripted. After two warriors manhandled him to the center circle, ripping from him his tunic and exposing his hideous gut for all to see, Galeo from his knees begged for mercy, his hands clasped together in prayer. He offered money he didn't have, offered favors from people who no longer favored him. He was mocked. He was jeered, and Philo allowed much time for all present to help him destroy what little was left of Tacitus Galeo.

"Your helmet, please." It was the helmet of the Secutor. Philo took it in hand, placed it atop his Emperor's bloodied sword and held it high. "Citizens of Rome, I do this honor for Ovid of Thebes. Ovid the Annihilator. Ovid, the mightiest of warriors. The most courageous, most skilled gladiator of our time. We, together, you and I, do this in remembrance of him."

I do not know how many tears fell besides mine when Philo placed Secutor's helmet upon his head, but I guarantee they could not be counted. With walking stick planted forward next to his left foot, Philo stepped back with his right foot and pierced the air. An Emperor's sword cleanly impaled the gut of Tacitus Galeo, its blood-dripping point exiting the small of his back. He clutched his hands tightly to the blade, severing his own fingers. He wheezed. He gurgled liquids of bile and blood. He glared with eyes wide open to the man holding the sword of his doom, the man twisting its handle to efficiently carve his innards, but Tacitus received nothing back -- no expression of anger or vindictiveness or regret or pity, not even pleasure, for all Tacitus Galeo saw staring back at him were two tiny holes, cold and black. The eyes of death. The eyes of a tortured Secutor.

A Gathering of the Good

Unlike the games for Vespasian, this day for Scipio ended long before shadows dimmed the arena floor. Emperor Aurelian did not wait for the return of his sword, making his exit through tunnel before his sword emerged from the still-gurgling Galeo. As for me, I had work to do. There were gladiators back at the Ludus Magnus waiting for me. Those who could be saved received surgeries, those who could not received comforts for pain until their end.

"How much longer will you be?" came a voice from behind me. Finishing a final stitch, I turned to see Gemellus and Antonia Siculus.

"An hour if you care to help me. Half an hour if you don't."

"Oh, Artimos," beamed Antonia. "You are the luckiest man alive."

"Why? Because I like the smell of blood?"

"No, silly. Philo. He's magnificent!"

"Don't I know it." I returned to my work with the last man who could be helped. "Were you pleased with our show?"

"So ecstatic we're giving a party," answered Gemellus. "And you're coming with us."

"Don't you think it rude to make everybody wait for me? By the way, have you seen Philo?"

"No to the first question; yes to the second." Antonia moved across from me opposite the table where I sewed together calf muscle of a split wide open leg. "We told our guests to come around five. As for Philo, you better keep a closer eye on him before somebody steals him away from you."

"Don't even suggest it. I'm past the point of return. Could never survive without him."

"No need to worry, Artimos," Gemellus assured while joining his wife to watch me stitch gladiator skin back together. "He's on loan. That's all."

"He's with Octavia," added the lady. "You remember. Livilla's sister. After all, Philo is a hero to them."

"What about me?"

"Artimos, darling. You were a hero long before any of this happened. Now, you're simply yesterday's news."

"Our Emperor doesn't think so."

"Wasn't that a treat? I assume he spoke with both of you?"

"Yes it was and yes he did." Finished with leg, I moved to my patient's forearm to seal a minor slice. "Most of what he said confused me, though. What did our intervention have to do with Galeo's shoddy construction materials scheme?"

Gemellus fielded my question. "He needed to raise a huge sum of money in order to secure the contract. Time was against him, so he arranged his wife's murder."

"Oh, I see. To get her death benefit."

"Exactly. All he had to do was wait for Ovid and Livilla to... you know, do it, and then he could make it appear Ovid killed her before killing himself."

"And Ovid spoiled it by killing the assassin. How sad." There was silence, and I suspected they thought I'd made a tasteless joke, which I had not. "You two know me better than that. I mean it. How incredibly tragic it is that a beautiful woman had to die, that a glorious man had to be destroyed, just so Galeo could line his pockets with public funds."

"Damned fool," Gemellus agreed. "A damned, greedy fool. Any man with an ounce of sense would have ended it himself. Saved us from all this trouble. I think Aurelian handled it beautifully, though. Don't you?"

"Without question. Everybody involved has to feel a degree of satisfaction."

Antonia confirmed my thought. "Euripides himself could not have written a better drama. And your Philo gave a stupendous performance. My great, great, great..."

"Antonia, please," chided her husband. "Just say Scipio. You will confuse yourself trying to remember."

"Artimos, how much longer?"

"Three more loops... one... two... three. There! Are you happy?"

"Come on. My carpentum waits."

"Her carpentum. Did you hear that, Artimos? Apparently we are to walk behind her like slaves."

"Men are slaves, Gemellus. Will always be."

"Some men aren't." Antonia circled the table and hugged me, staining herself from my bloody clothing. "See, Artimos? I said you were the luckiest man alive."

At their home I bathed, and while Gemellus and Antonia bathed together I ate a small snack, small because that is all they allowed me. Outfitted with casual cream-colored tunic provided by near-to-my-size Gemellus, I joined them again in Antonia's carpentum for my ride to their party.

"So, where are we going?"

"Never you mind," Antonia teased. "If you don't trust us by now we'll throw you out and you can walk home."

Through the city gates, past the Servian Wall, I personally was growing tired of the Via Ostiensis. The carpentum conversation stopped altogether, a hint that Mr. and Mrs. Siculus were up to no good, which in my experience had always ended up being something very good. We parked in front of the Ostia Harbor Grain Exchange amongst many, many, many carpentums. They entered ahead of me, and the scene inside astonished beyond belief.

The tired wooden floor was refinished to its beautiful oak shine from corner to corner, ceiling as well. Two hundred years of grime had disappeared and the whiteness of dolomite in stone walls nearly blinded the eye. All was illuminated by wall torches bracketed by glowing silver fixtures, plus a handsome and huge chandelier of iron suspended by long chain from ceiling.

And the people! Antonia's family was there. Gemellus's family was there. Octavia and Livilla's family; Drusus Macarius and Vittelius Silanus; Argo Baltius and his wife; Lucinius Aulus and his; Frontenus Nervo and his, both sporting smiles of happiness, their arms wrapped to one another, confirmation that my skin-conditioning cream doubled as an effective healer of a fractured marriage; Nervo's daughter and his employees and their families and seemingly everybody who had attended the Scipio games; all were there dining from tables filled with foodstuffs and drinking from bars serving ales and wines.

Everything was new. Everything was perfect. Everything was so Antonia.

She deserved at least a hug. "When on earth did you do all of this?"

"Octavia and I began as soon as you sent over the papers. Do you like it?"

"Good god, yes. It's as though the Julio-Claudians have returned to entertain us."

"Can't you just feel the history of it? Augustus himself may have walked these floors for all we know."

"Let's just say that he did."

"You haven't seen the best of it. Come."

She led me to the back room. Where once had been the tiny trap door steps of boards now was floor cut open to a grand staircase of matching oak, twice the width of the old and framed by handsomely polished mahogany bannisters. Antonia and I descended with arms hooked, Gemellus behind us and all others moving to follow. No need to duck my head as before, I was presented with not a dark, damp basement, but a palace, walls of stone fronted by new walls of stucco with murals too detailed for one to absorb at first glance. The once filthy stone floor shined of whiteness like the walls above, lit by bracketed torches like those above. That little commode hole now was a full-sized two-holer with bath tub large enough for at least two. And the water, I could hear its trickle.

But with all the niceties surrounding me, what stood out most were the three items left over from the bad old days: the torture table; the suspension chains; the cross of t. And here, standing near the cross with walking stick in one hand and drink in the other, was Philo.

He spoke with a man unknown to me. In fact, none of the men gathered in this room were known to me, but when Philo turned to acknowledge my presence with his ever-inviting smile, all else was oblivious to me.

I joined him, and much to my surprise he kissed me, embarrassed me.

"Philo!" I whispered. "Careful. What will others think?"

"No thinking. They will know. As they should know. As you should know."

And with that, I embraced him for a seriously wet kiss to leave no doubts.

"Look, Artimos." He pointed to the cross. "You're just in time for the show."

Laying atop the wood on the stone floor with arms stretched and roped to patibulum, ankles bound together on the stipes, a naked man was awaiting his ascension, his muscular body enhanced with short black hair. Covering his head was the Secutor's helmet. What did he feel? I could not know. He wanted to escape. His straining muscles and expanding chest told me that much, but he knew there would be no escape, as did I.

Naked and beautiful male servants raised him. Ropes threaded through metal eye-hooks imbedded atop the cross ran to pulleys bolted to the ceiling rafters. They pulled the ropes and the cross slowly ascended to vertical. They positioned the foot of the stipes at a hole bored into stone floor and dropped him with a painful thud. He groaned, the pace of his breathing quickened, and gravity tortured him.

"I reckon with his strength, and with this form of crucifixion, he's good for a couple of hours... maybe three."

Philo spoke coldly, as though such an agonizing death meant nothing, and then I realized from his body whose tormented face was hidden beneath the Secutor's mask.

"Timor?"

"In the flesh. He's quite handsome if you cover those ape-man jowls."

"He's glorious. You must have trimmed his body hair from simian length to human."

Our slave truly was a sight to behold. Every muscle and line of his strength bulged to capacity, and as the pressure intensified on his rib cage and his breathing became more and more shallow, his heart increased its vain attempts to circulate his oxygen-deprived blood. This caused his phallus to inflate. It sprang to full erection, majestically piercing the air with horizontal precision.

"Philo, is there anything more beautiful than this? A man on the cross? Naked? Helplessly stretched and exposed for all to see?"

"No. Nothing compares."

"I am tempted to ravage him."

"Do. That's why we brought him here."

"But what will the others... "

I scanned the room to find it empty. Just Philo, me, and our crucified man. The murals fascinated me. Painted upon one wall was Scipio at the Zama battlefield, his triumphant foot atop the chest of a fallen Hannibal, terrified elephants scattering in all directions. Another wall depicted

Valentinian, his...

Artimos!

Yes, Philo.

We are not there yet. Careful what you say. After all, I don't remember that room as being so grand. They merely cleaned it up, built the stairwell and bath and new pipes to connect us with water.

It is grand, Philo. It is because I say so. Persophone brings us here for our anniversary. How many years now?

Years? There are no years. Only numbers and words. Look, Artimos, your opportunity to ravage Timor has passed. All of our friends have returned.

I don't know these people.

They know you. They are Romans. Men of greatness. Men of integrity. Men who did the best they could for their fellow citizens.

The good Emperors?

Correct, but not just Emperors. All good Romans, Emperors, or nobodies like us, before us and after us. Should I introduce them?

No. It will take forever.

We have forever. My god, man! Rome lasted a thousand years. We only lived there for 60.

That time.

Yes, that time, but since you cannot let go of your concerns with time, I'll just categorize them as those who follow the Artimos religion.

And is it a true religion?

We are not allowed to tell it. You know that. If we did, people would be tempted to take short cuts. Besides, it might scare them to death.

Then they could join our party.

Only if they follow your religion.

That is answer enough.

Speaking of enough, Timor's had it. Let's take him down and go on our way.

Timor made us a good sum of money in his day. Didn't he, Philo? Should I tell it? We can't just leave the story hanging.

I'll tell it precisely: Our secretive monthly banquets at the Ostia Harbor Grain Exchange quickly became the social event to beat all. Come to the extravaganza! See the tortured Secutor. Touch him. Taste him. Inject yourself with his manly strength.

Our reservation fees were piffle, but good people were so thrilled with our show they lavished us with donations upon leaving. Timor performed as though a human god whether he was on the cross, suspension chains or torture table, and his masculine body was ravaged by all who cared to partake, just as Artimos suggested be done. The program rotated every month -- one for men, the next for marrieds, the third for women. And of course, we invested our money by carefully choosing two more he-man slaves to expand customer options and increase flow of semen.

As for other investments, we turned those over to Frontenus Nervo. In exchange for his one-third ownership of our building he gave us one-third percentage of his trading company, and when our nest egg was more than could be spent in a lifetime, Artimos retired from the Ludus Magnus. We purchased a villa in Ephesus. We took our men with us for

OUR enjoyment. Their lives as slaves were more pleasant than most freedmen could claim, free born men for that matter.

And because many still find death depressing even though they shouldn't, I will end our story here. Don't want to tempt myself towards mush, and besides...

Philo, I would like to add one final note.

Do.

I believe Philo would have one day walked without his stick had Galeo not further damaged what was already fragile. As a result, the pain of his full weight upon twice-damaged bone...

Artimos! I used my stick because I liked it. It came from you, so when I touched it you were always with me.

My! You are both cock-sure and forgetful. I am moved by your sentiment, Philo, but still say you could not have walked without your stick.

Now you've done it. We quarrel, Persephone fidgets.

So I see. She beckons us to drink.

Then quickly, Artimos, kiss me.

Consider it done.

The Tortured Secutor

A Boner Book

ABOUT THE AUTHOR

Jardonn Smith is the instigator of the BDSM web site Jardonn's Erotic Tales.com, where you'll also find the audio MP3 erotica of his Uncle Jasper and writings of cousin Jack. Together, the three of them tell their adventures of straight, gay and bisexual activities.

Jardonn sees his men as god-like, heroic creatures, and he insists they be bound to their altars in order to receive his praise. It is the only proper method in which to glorify the beauty of the male physique.

Jardonn Smith is also the author of:

I'll Never Talk: Erotic Tales of Defiant Men

The Bishop of Grunewald: A Tale from the Dungeon

Liquid Delights: Erotic Tales of Wetness

Elevated Lust

Available at Goodboner.com, jardonnserotictales.com
or your local bookstore.

www.ingramcontent.com/pod-product-compliance
Lightning Source LLC
Chambersburg PA
CBHW070800280626
47162CB00016B/1570